Grilled Corruption:

Burnt Ends Mysteries

Book 2

Erica J Whelton

Publisher: Sunseri Design Publishing
ISBN: 978-1-956069-39-6

Printed in the United States of America

To my husband who has supported me in my dreams and continues to support me. Also, he inspired the cooking competition for this story.

.

Chapter One

The Australian Cattle Dog moved with the focused intensity of a natural-born athlete, his blue-speckled coat gleaming in the late afternoon Hill Country sun. Jackie Prescott watched from the new covered pavilion as Blue, Tom Whitfield's pride and joy, guided three sheep around a series of orange cones with the precision of a seasoned professional.

"Easy, Blue. That'll do," Tom called out, and the dog immediately dropped into a crouch, his intelligent eyes never leaving the small flock. A crowd of about thirty people, mostly families with children and a few tourists with cameras, applauded appreciatively from the tiered wooden bleachers they'd installed last month.

"How does he make it look so effortless?" asked a little girl in the front row, her voice carrying across the demonstration area.

Tom's weathered face broke into a genuine smile. "Well, darlin', Blue here's been working sheep and cattle since he was just a pup. It's what his breed was born to do. These dogs can cover twenty-five miles a day on a ranch, keeping livestock safe and where they need to be."

Jackie felt a warm sense of satisfaction watching the scene unfold. Six months ago, Tom Whitfield had been their biggest antagonist, sabotaging their business in a misguided attempt to protect them from danger.

Now he was drawing weekend crowds to their expanded restaurant grounds with educational demonstrations that perfectly complemented their mission of honoring Hill Country agricultural traditions.

The transformation hadn't happened overnight. It had taken weeks of careful conversations, shared meals, and mutual respect building before they all agreed to their partnership. But once he'd committed, he'd thrown himself into the project with the same intense focus he brought to everything else.

"The key to working with a herding dog," Tom continued, walking among the audience as Blue maintained his vigilant watch over the sheep, "is understanding that you're not commanding the animal. You're communicating with a partner who's probably smarter than you are and definitely has better instincts."

"Is that why you don't raise your voice at him?" asked a teenage boy.

"Exactly right. Blue and I, we've developed our own language over the years. A whistle means one thing, a hand signal means another. Shouting just confuses the message and scares the livestock."

Jackie smiled, remembering how Tom's communication style had improved dramatically since they'd started working together. The man who used to express concern through cattle-based harassment now ran weekend workshops on sustainable ranching practices, told stories about four generations of Whitfield family history, and patiently answered questions from city kids who'd never seen a working dog in action.

After the demonstration, as the crowd dispersed and families headed toward the restaurant for early dinner, Melody approached the herding area with the careful, measured steps Jackie had learned to recognize when her niece was processing something new.

"Tom," Melody said, stopping at what appeared to be a precisely calculated distance from Blue, "I've been researching Australian Cattle Dogs since we scheduled the herding demonstrations. I wanted to understand proper interaction protocols for working dogs."

Tom's weathered face broke into a genuine smile. "Protocols?"

"Yes. I learned that working dogs require different interaction approaches than pet dogs. They have higher intelligence levels, stronger prey drives, and specific behavioral cues that shouldn't be disrupted." Melody consulted a small notebook she'd pulled from her pocket. "Australian Cattle Dogs specifically are bred for independence and problem-solving, with heightened spatial awareness and pack hierarchy sensitivity."

Blue had been lying in his resting position near Tom's feet, but as Melody spoke, the dog's ears pricked forward and he lifted his head, studying her with the same intense focus he'd shown with the sheep.

"He's listening to you," Tom observed with interest.

"I also researched proper greeting behavior," Melody continued, still maintaining her careful distance. "I should avoid direct eye contact initially, let him approach me rather than approaching him, and keep my voice calm and steady. Working dogs respond better to confident, predictable behavior."

"You've done your homework," Tom said, clearly impressed. "Most people just want to rush up and pet him without thinking about what that means to a dog who's trained to read intentions and protect his territory."

Blue rose to his feet, not in an aggressive stance but with alert curiosity, his intelligent eyes fixed on Melody. After a moment of what looked like assessment, he took two deliberate steps toward her, then sat and tilted his head in a distinctly questioning gesture.

"He's asking permission," Tom said quietly. "I've never seen him do that with a stranger before."

Melody's systematic preparation hadn't accounted for this possibility. "Permission for what?"

"To get to know you. Blue's got good instincts about people. He can sense when someone's... different. Not in a bad way," Tom added quickly, "but different in ways that matter to him."

Melody looked down at Blue, who was now sitting perfectly still about four feet away, his posture patient and respectful. "May I try the greeting protocol I researched?"

"Go ahead. But I think you can trust your instincts more than your research with this one."

Melody slowly lowered herself to a crouch, making herself less imposing while keeping her movements deliberate and predictable. She extended one hand, palm down, and waited.

Blue approached with careful steps, his body language completely non-threatening. He sniffed her hand briefly, then, in a gesture that surprised everyone watching, he gently pressed his head against her palm and sighed a deep, contented sound.

"Well, I'll be," Tom murmured. "He's never done that before. Blue's polite with visitors, but he doesn't usually seek out physical contact with people he's just met."

Melody felt an unexpected warmth spread through her chest as Blue settled beside her, close enough that she could feel his calm breathing. "Why do you think he's responding to me this way?"

"Working dogs are bred to read everything including body language, energy, and intentions. They pick up on things most people miss." Tom settled on a nearby hay bale, watching the interaction with fascination. "Blue can probably sense that you process the world differently. Some animals are drawn to that kind of unique awareness."

"You mean my autism?"

"I mean the way you see details other people miss, the way you think through problems systematically, the way you're calm and deliberate in your movements. Those are exactly the qualities Blue respects in his work."

Melody found herself gently stroking Blue's head, surprised by how soothing the repetitive motion felt. "He's remarkably calm for a high-energy breed."

"He knows when to be intense and when to be still. Right now, he's decided his job is to be still with you." Tom's voice carried genuine warmth. "You've got a gift with him, Melody. Not everyone can earn a working dog's respect that quickly."

Jackie watched from the pavilion as her niece and Blue settled into comfortable companionship, Melody's usual tension visibly easing as the dog pressed against her side. It was the most relaxed she'd seen Melody with any new situation in months.

"Tom," Melody said after several minutes of quiet companionship, "would it be appropriate for me to spend time with Blue during his rest periods? I think I'd like to learn more about his training methods and behavioral patterns."

"I think Blue would like that very much," Tom replied. "And I'd enjoy having someone around who appreciates the science behind what he does. Most people just see the show, but you understand there's real intelligence and methodology involved."

Melody said goodbye so Tom could get ready for his next demonstration.

"Aunt Jackie?" Melody called out. "We need to make a decision about the competition invitation. The registration deadline is tomorrow."

Jackie watched as Melody walked over to the picnic table she had been previously sitting at, grabbing a thick envelope and wearing the expression she got when she was working through complex logistics in her head.

At twenty-two, Melody had grown more confident over the past six months, though she still preferred to approach new situations with careful analysis and detailed planning, just like she had with the dog. It was everything in her life that was approached that way.

"Let's find your mom and talk it through," Jackie suggested, though she was pretty sure she already knew what Lauren's answer would be. Her sister had been practically vibrating with excitement ever since the invitation arrived three days ago.

They found Lauren in the main restaurant, wiping down tables after the lunch rush while humming something that sounded suspiciously upbeat. Clearly she was thinking about Sheriff Ray Martinez.

The pair had been on several dates over the past six months. Not as many as either would like, but it was all they could manage given her restaurant duties and Ray's duties as sheriff.

The dining room had been expanded twice since they'd inherited the place, but it still maintained the warm, welcoming atmosphere that Uncle Charlie Joe had created. Photographs of customers and community events covered the walls, and the smell of hickory smoke drifted in from the outdoor kitchen where Jovie was tending the afternoon brisket. There were the originals from Charlie Joe, but now a bunch of the new owners and changes were showcased.

"So," Jackie said, settling at their usual corner table, "are we really going to enter a barbecue competition?"

Lauren's face lit up like Christmas morning. "The Fourth Annual Hill Country Barbecue Championship! Right here in Prairie Rose! We'd be crazy not to enter."

The invitation had come through the mail a month or so ago, and they had yet to make a decision. With the deadline looming they had to decide once and for all.

"We'd be crazy to enter," Jackie countered, though without real heat. "We're restaurant cooks, not competition pitmasters. There's a huge difference."

"Jovie competed in barbecue contests for fifteen years," Lauren pointed out. "She's offered to coach us. And think about the exposure with the food bloggers, regional media, potential customers from all over Texas."

Melody opened the envelope and spread the registration materials across the table. "The competition categories are brisket, ribs, pulled pork, and chicken. Entry fee is three hundred dollars per team, with a first prize of ten thousand dollars and a trophy."

"Ten thousand dollars?" Jackie raised an eyebrow.

"Plus, regional recognition and possible sponsorship opportunities," Lauren added quickly. "Some of these pitmasters have turned competition wins into restaurant chains, TV shows, product lines."

"Though I doubt Wade Brooks will be happy to see us competing," Lauren added with a slight frown. "He stopped by last week asking pointed questions about our entry plans."

"Wade Brooks?" Jackie asked.

"Owns Brooks' Barbecue Barn over in Cedar Hill," Jovie explained, joining their conversation. "He and Charlie Joe had a rivalry going back twenty years. Wade's never gotten over the fact that Charlie Joe's place became the regional destination while his stayed local."

"What kind of questions was he asking?" Melody wanted to know.

"Whether we had 'proper experience' for competition level barbecue, if we understood the 'commitment required,' that sort of thing. But his tone suggested he hoped we'd decide not to compete."

Jackie studied the registration forms, noting the long list of rules, regulations, and equipment requirements. "This isn't just cooking, Lauren. It's a highly structured competition with specific protocols, time limits, and presentation requirements. Are we really equipped for that level of pressure?"

"We handle pressure every Sunday when we serve two hundred people for community dinner," Lauren said. "We've catered events for three hundred. We know how to cook good barbecue under time constraints."

"Restaurant service is different from competition judging," Jackie pointed out. "Our customers know us. They're rooting for us to succeed. Competition judges are looking for technical perfection and consistency."

"The competition judging uses a standardized scoring system," Melody said, reading from the regulations. "Appearance, taste, and tenderness, each scored from six to nine points. Teams are judged blindly. Judges don't know which entry belongs to which competitor."

"Which means our reputation won't help or hurt us," Lauren said. "It'll be purely about the quality of our barbecue."

Jackie looked around the restaurant they'd built together, thinking about how much their lives had changed in less than a year. The three of them were still living above the restaurant and it worked perfectly for them.

Her divorce from Richard was final, her law practice was officially closed, and for the first time in decades, she woke up each morning excited about the day ahead.

But competition barbecue felt like a different world entirely, with risks they hadn't fully considered.

"What does Jovie think about our chances?" Jackie asked.

"She thinks we have excellent fundamentals but need intensive coaching on competition-specific techniques," Melody replied. "She's already created a training schedule that would prepare us for the event."

The front door chimed, and Maria Santos entered carrying a tray of what looked like cookies. "Afternoon, ladies. My grandmother's praline cookies for the weekend dessert special." She paused, noticing the spread of competition materials. "Y'all thinking about entering the championship?"

"We're discussing it," Jackie said diplomatically.

"You should do it," Maria said immediately. "This town's been needing something to put us on the map besides that old murder business. A local team in the barbecue championship would be perfect."

"See?" Lauren said triumphantly. "Even Maria thinks it's a good idea."

"Maria also thought it was a good idea when you decided to add venison burgers to the menu," Jackie reminded her.

"Hey, the venison burgers were popular," Lauren protested. "We sold out every weekend until hunting season ended."

Through the window, Jackie could see Tom's second demonstration wrapping up. Blue was guiding the sheep back to their temporary pen while children asked if they could pet him and parents took final photos. The scene embodied everything they'd worked to create. A place where tradition and community intersected, where people could learn something new while enjoying excellent food.

Maybe the competition could be part of that mission.

"Alright," Jackie said finally. "Let's talk to Jovie. If she thinks we can be competitive, and if she's willing to coach us properly, we'll give it a shot."

"Really?" Lauren's eyes sparkled with excitement.

"Really. But," Jackie held up a hand, "we do this right. Professional preparation, proper equipment, realistic expectations. This isn't just about having fun, it's about representing our restaurant and our community."

"And about learning new techniques that could improve our regular menu offerings," Melody added, ever practical.

"Plus, think about the stories we'll be able to tell," Lauren said. "Win or lose, this could be an amazing experience."

Jackie signed the registration forms before she could change her mind. "Okay, Jovie better know what she's getting us into."

As if summoned by her name, Jovie appeared from the kitchen, wiping her hands on her apron and looking pleased about something. "I just heard Tom telling his audience that we've got the best brisket in the Hill Country. Had at least six people ask about booking catering for their events."

"Speaking of brisket," Lauren said, "we just registered for the barbecue championship."

Jovie's face broke into a wide grin. "About time! I was starting to think y'all were all talk and no action. When do we start training?"

"Training?" Jackie asked.

"Honey, competition barbecue is like Olympic cooking. You don't just show up and wing it. We've got three weeks to get you ready to face some of the best pitmasters in Texas." Jovie pulled up a chair and cracked her knuckles. "Good thing I love a challenge."

As the afternoon sun slanted through the restaurant windows, Jackie felt the familiar thrill of embarking on something new and slightly terrifying. Six months ago, she'd been a burned-out divorce attorney with no family connections and no sense of purpose.

Now she was about to enter a barbecue competition with her sister and niece, coached by a woman who'd become like family.

Uncle Charlie Joe would probably be laughing his head off at the idea of his city-lawyer great-niece competing against professional pitmasters. But he'd also be proud that they were willing to take risks, to push themselves beyond their comfort zones in service of the community he'd loved.

"So, when do we meet our competition?" Jackie asked.

"Some of them will be scouting our restaurant over the next few weeks," Jovie said. "Word travels fast in the barbecue world. Once your registration becomes public, every serious competitor will want to taste what they're up against."

"They'll be eating here? Checking us out?" Lauren asked.

"Count on it. Competition pitmasters take their research seriously. They'll come in as regular customers, order everything on the menu, and take mental notes about our techniques, our seasoning, our presentation style."

Melody looked up from the competition rules she was still studying. "So, we'll be competing against people who have inside knowledge of our food?"

"Which is why we need to develop some new techniques that won't be on display in our regular menu," Jovie said with a gleam in her eye. "Secret weapons, if you will."

Jackie laughed. "Six months ago, I was defending white-collar criminals, and now I'm plotting secret barbecue strategies. My life has gotten so much weirder."

"Better weird than boring," Lauren said firmly.

As Tom's demonstration crowd began to disperse and the restaurant prepared for the evening rush, Jackie felt a deep contentment settle over her. This was her life now unexpected, challenging, filled with people she cared about and work that mattered.

The competition would test them in new ways, but they'd face it together. And if Uncle Charlie Joe had taught them anything, it was that family could overcome just about any challenge when they stuck together.

Even if that challenge involved facing off against legendary pitmasters for a ten-thousand-dollar prize and regional bragging rights.

"Alright, coach," Jackie said to Jovie. "What's our first lesson?"

Chapter Two

The next morning arrived with the kind of cool breezy April air that made the Hill Country famous, Jackie went down to meet Jovie at her normal 5 am. But instead of her usual prep work, Jovie had transformed the outdoor kitchen into what looked like a military training ground for barbecue.

"Morning, soldier," Jovie said with a grin, gesturing to a table covered with notebooks, timers, thermometers, and what appeared to be a detailed schematic of a competition setup. "Ready to learn what real barbecue competition looks like?"

Jackie poured herself coffee from the pot Jovie had already started. She had a feeling she'd need this to get through the morning. "I thought I knew what real barbecue looked like. We serve it every day."

"Restaurant barbecue and competition barbecue are different animals," Jovie said, opening one of the notebooks. "Restaurant cooking is about consistency and volume. Competition cooking is about perfection in small batches. Every ounce of meat has to be flawless."

Lauren and Melody joined them, both looking more alert than anyone should at 5 AM. Melody carried her own notebook and had clearly been doing research.

"I found seventeen YouTube channels dedicated to competition barbecue," Melody announced. "Also, fourteen books, forty-three blog posts, and a statistical analysis of winning techniques from the past five years."

"Of course you did," Jackie said fondly. "What did you learn?"

"That we're about to enter a highly technical field with established masters who've been perfecting their craft for decades." Melody consulted her notes. "The margin of error for winning entries is typically less than half a point across all judging categories."

"Half a point?" Lauren asked. "That's like the difference between perfect and almost perfect?"

"Exactly," Jovie confirmed. "Which is why we're going to spend the next three weeks drilling every aspect of technique until you can execute flawlessly under pressure."

She opened her notebook to reveal pages of handwritten recipes, timing charts, and technique descriptions. "I competed seriously for fifteen years. That was before I got divorced and had a young child to support. Won regional championships in brisket and ribs, placed in the top ten at the state level three times."

Jackie looked at Jovie with new respect. "You never mentioned that."

"Charlie Joe knew. He hired me because he wanted someone who understood both restaurant cooking and competition level technique." Jovie's expression grew fond. "He said I was overqualified to work in a small town barbecue joint, but I told him I was exactly where I needed to be."

"That's so nice of him. He knew talent," Jackie said.

"So, what's our first lesson?" Lauren asked, rolling up her sleeves.

"Temperature control," Jovie said immediately. "Competition judges are looking for meat that's cooked to exact doneness. Not close, not good enough but exact. That means understanding how different cuts respond to heat, how weather affects cooking times, and how to adjust for equipment variations."

She led them to the main smoker, which looked different than usual. Additional thermometers had been installed at various points, and a new digital monitoring system displayed temperatures from multiple locations within the cooking chamber.

"Restaurant smoking aims for a temperature range," Jovie explained. "Competition smoking aims for a specific temperature, maintained consistently throughout the cook. Watch this."

She made a small adjustment to the air vents, and Jackie watched the digital display shift from 247 degrees to 250 degrees exactly.

"Three-degree difference?" Lauren asked.

"Three degrees can mean the difference between meat that's tender and meat that's perfect," Jovie said. "And perfect is what wins competitions."

For the next hour, they practiced temperature control until Jackie felt confident she could maintain 250 degrees plus or minus one degree for extended periods. It was more challenging than she'd expected, requiring constant attention to wind direction, fuel management, and air flow.

"This is just the beginning," Jovie warned. "Tomorrow we'll work on seasoning techniques, then trimming, then presentation. By the end of three weeks, you'll be able to produce competition-quality barbecue in your sleep."

They were deep into a lesson on proper brisket trimming when a pickup truck pulled into the parking lot. Jackie looked up to see a tall man in his late sixties climbing out of the vehicle, moving with the easy confidence of someone comfortable in his own skin.

"That's Tex Morrison," Jovie said quietly, her voice carrying a note of respect that Jackie had rarely heard from her. "Legendary pitmaster, competition judge, and the closest thing our world has to royalty."

The man approaching them was impressive even at a distance with his silver hair under a well-worn cowboy hat, boots that had seen serious use, and the kind of presence that suggested he was used to commanding attention. As he got closer, Jackie noticed his resemblance to Tom Whitfield around the eyes and jawline.

"Morning, ladies," Tex Morrison said, his voice carrying a slight Texas drawl that seemed authentic rather than forced. "I'm Tex Morrison, one of the judges for the championship. Heard y'all registered yesterday, thought I'd stop by and introduce myself."

"Mr. Morrison," Jovie said, standing up straighter. "This is an honor. Jackie and Lauren Prescott, and Melody Beniot. They own the restaurant."

Tex shook hands with each of them, his grip firm but not overwhelming. "Please, call me Tex. And I hear Jovie Barber's coaching you. That's smart. She was one of the toughest competitors on the circuit back in her day."

"You know Jovie's work?" Jackie asked.

"Know it? I judged her entries at least a dozen times. She had a brisket technique that was pure poetry, and her ribs could make you weep with joy." Tex's expression grew respectful. "She's the reason I always tell young pitmasters that technical skill matters more than expensive equipment."

Jovie blushed slightly. "Tex Morrison taught half the champions in Texas, either directly or through people he mentored. If he says something about barbecue, you listen."

"Speaking of listening," Tex said, "mind if I try some of your regular menu? I like to get a sense of a team's baseline capabilities before the competition."

"Of course," Lauren said immediately. "What would you like to try?"

"Brisket sandwich, lean and fatty mixed, with your regular sides. And sweet tea if you've got it." Tex settled at one of the picnic tables under the oak tree. "Take your time. I'm not in a hurry."

As Lauren headed to the kitchen to prepare Tex's order, Jovie continued the training session, but Jackie noticed her movements were more precise, her explanations more detailed. Having a legend watching them practice had clearly raised the stakes.

"Melody," Tex called out, "you're taking notes pretty seriously there. Planning to compete yourself?"

"I'm documenting the learning process," Melody replied without looking up from her notebook. "Optimal knowledge retention requires systematic recording of new information."

"Smart approach. Competition barbecue is about details, and the teams that keep the best records usually have the most consistent results." Tex leaned back in his chair. "So, I hear from my cousin that he does demos here on the weekends?"

"You mean Tom? He's your cousin?" Jackie asked.

"Yep, Tom's a good man, just took him a while to figure out how to show it properly." Tex chuckled. "Whitfield men have always been better with cattle than with people, but they're loyal once you earn their respect."

Lauren returned with Tex's order, setting it down with the kind of careful presentation they used for their regular customers. Tex took his time examining the brisket before tasting it, chewing thoughtfully and making small notes in a pocket notebook.

"This is excellent restaurant barbecue," he said finally. "Good smoke flavor, proper tenderness, well-balanced seasoning. You've got solid fundamentals."

"But?" Jackie asked, hearing the unspoken qualification.

"But restaurant barbecue and competition barbecue are different standards. This brisket would satisfy any customer and keep them coming back. Competition brisket has to be flawless in ways most customers would never notice." Tex took another bite, considering. "The good news is, you've got the foundation. The challenging news is you need to build about six more layers on top of that foundation."

"What kinds of layers?" Lauren asked.

"Perfect moisture content, precise texture, optimal fat rendering, exact seasoning balance, and presentation that looks like art." Tex finished his sandwich with obvious enjoyment. "Plus, you need to do all of that under time pressure, in front of crowds, with judges who've tasted the best barbecue in the world."

"Are we crazy for thinking we can compete?" Jackie asked directly.

Tex was quiet for a moment, studying each of them carefully. "Most folks who enter their first competition are crazy for thinking they can win. But competing? Learning? Testing yourselves against serious standards? That's not crazy at all."

He stood up, dropping money on the table, which was twice what the meal cost. "Besides, Jovie's coaching you, and she knows what it takes. Listen to her, practice obsessively, and don't worry about winning your first time out. Focus on not embarrassing yourselves, and you'll probably surprise everyone."

"Including ourselves?" Melody asked.

"Especially yourselves." Tex tipped his hat to them. "Looking forward to tasting your competition entries, ladies. And Jovie? It's good to see you back in the game, even as a coach."

After Tex drove away, the four women sat in contemplative silence.

"He seems nice," Lauren said finally.

"He's a legend," Jovie corrected. "Tex Morrison has forgotten more about barbecue than most people ever learn. If he thinks we have potential, that's significant."

"He also made it clear we're not ready yet," Jackie pointed out.

"Of course, we're not ready yet. That's why we have three weeks of intensive training ahead of us." Jovie stood up and clapped her hands together. "Break time's over. Let's get back to work."

As they resumed their temperature control practice, Jackie found herself thinking about Tex Morrison's assessment. Excellent restaurant barbecue, but not competition ready. It was an honest evaluation that neither crushed their confidence nor gave them false hope.

"Jovie," she said, adjusting the smoker vents with new precision, "when you were competing, how did you know you were ready?"

"When I stopped thinking about each step and started feeling the barbecue," Jovie replied. "When I could tell by the sound of the sizzle whether the heat was right, when I could judge doneness by the way the meat moved when I poked it, when seasoning became instinct instead of measurement."

"How long did that take?"

"About five years of serious competition." Jovie grinned at Jackie's expression. "Don't worry. We're not aiming for mastery in three weeks. We're aiming for competence. That's achievable."

As the morning progressed, Jackie began to understand the difference between cooking barbecue and competing with barbecue. Every detail mattered in ways she'd never considered. The thickness of the smoke ring, the consistency of the bark, the internal temperature measured to tenths of degrees rather than the nearest five degrees.

It was intimidating and exhilarating at the same time.

By lunch time, they had a training schedule that would consume most of their free time for the next three weeks. Practice sessions every morning before the restaurant opened, technique refinement during slow periods, and full competition run-throughs on their days off.

"Are we really going to be ready?" Lauren asked as they prepared for the lunch rush.

"We're going to be as ready as three weeks of intensive training can make us," Jackie replied. "Whether that's ready enough, we'll find out."

"The statistical probability of winning is low for first-time competitors," Melody observed. "But the learning opportunity value is significant regardless of placement."

As customers began arriving for lunch, Jackie noticed herself looking at each plate with new eyes, evaluating not just whether it looked good but whether it met the exacting standards Tex Morrison had described. It was going to be a long three weeks, but she was looking forward to the challenge.

Jackie was pretty sure competition barbecue was about as far outside her comfort zone as she could get without leaving Texas entirely. But that was exactly why she was excited to try.

Chapter Three

The Fourth Annual Hill Country Barbecue Championship transformed Prairie Rose's main park into something Jackie had never imagined could exist in their quiet town. Dozens of massive smokers lined the grassy area like steel sentinels, each one tended by teams wearing matching shirts and expressions of intense concentration.

The air was thick with hickory, oak, pecan and mesquite smoke as each team had a different preference, and the sound of sizzling meat mixed with competitive banter and nervous laughter.

"This is incredible," Lauren breathed, taking in the scene from their assigned cooking area.

They arrived at 4 AM to set up, but the park was already buzzing with activity. Some teams had clearly been there since midnight, their briskets already hours into the long cooking process.

Jackie felt a familiar flutter of performance anxiety as she surveyed their competition. These weren't weekend backyard grillers. These were serious pitmasters with custom equipment, professional setups, and the kind of easy confidence that came from years of experience.

"Team Smoke and Mirrors from Austin," Melody read from her notebook, pointing to an elaborate setup with three different smokers and what looked like a small army of assistants. "They've won the state championship twice in the past five years."

"Lone Star Barbecue Company from San Antonio," Jackie added, watching a team efficiently manage what appeared to be a full outdoor kitchen. "Their brisket was featured in Texas Monthly last year."

"And there's Wade Brooks with his Cedar Hill crew," Lauren said, nodding toward a setup about fifty yards away. "Brooks' Barbecue Barn. They've got quite the operation."

Jackie looked over to see a heavyset man in his fifties directing three younger men in matching red shirts. Wade Brooks had the kind of aggressive confidence that came from years of local success, but Jackie noticed how he kept glancing in their direction with obvious disapproval.

"He's been watching us since we arrived," Melody observed. "Statistical frequency of his glances suggests either professional curiosity or personal animosity."

"Definitely personal animosity," Jovie said quietly. "Wade's been telling people around town that 'outsiders' shouldn't be competing in local events, that the competition should be for 'established' barbecue operations only."

"Well, we aren't outsiders any longer. We're part of Prairie Rose," Jackie said squaring her shoulders.

"That a girl!" Jovie cheered.

"Oh, there's Billy 'Smoke' Jackson from East Texas," Lauren observed, nodding toward a bearded man in his forties who was arguing loudly with one of his team members. "He's got quite a reputation, according to the internet research I did last night."

Jackie had heard of Smoke Jackson. His reputation extended beyond barbecue into general unpleasantness. He'd been banned from two competitions for unsportsmanlike conduct and was known for aggressive tactics both on and off the competition circuit.

"Nervous?" Jovie asked, joining them with an armload of supplies from their truck.

"Terrified," Jackie admitted. "These people are professionals. Look at that setup over there. They've got more equipment than our entire restaurant."

"Equipment doesn't win competitions," Jovie said firmly. "Skill wins competitions. Heart wins competitions. And y'all have both."

Their own setup was modest but functional. One large smoker, two smaller ones for sides, and a prep table that Melody had organized with military precision. Everything they needed was within arm's reach, labeled, and arranged according to the timing schedule they'd practiced obsessively for three weeks.

"First call for chicken submission is at 3 PM," Melody announced, checking her watch. "Ribs at 4 PM, pulled pork at 5 PM, brisket at 6 PM. All entries must be submitted in regulation boxes with team numbers only. No identifying information."

"Plenty of time," Jovie said, though Jackie noticed she was checking the smoker temperature more frequently than usual. Even their experienced coach was feeling the pressure.

As the morning progressed, Jackie began to relax into the familiar rhythm of barbecue preparation. The techniques were the same ones they'd practiced, just with higher stakes and more critical evaluation. Their brisket was cooking beautifully, developing the deep bark and perfect smoke ring that Jovie had taught them to recognize.

Around 10 AM, when the morning setup was complete and their brisket was smoking beautifully, Jovie looked up from checking temperatures and smiled at someone approaching their station.

"Emma," she said, her voice filled with a warmth Jackie had rarely heard from their typically reserved cook. "You made it."

Jackie turned to see a young woman in her late twenties walking toward them, moving carefully but with obvious determination. She was thin in the way that suggested recent illness, but her eyes were bright and her smile genuine as she approached their setup.

"I told you I wouldn't miss your big comeback to competition cooking," Emma said, embracing her mother with the careful tenderness of someone who'd learned to be gentle with both giving and receiving affection.

"Emma, I'd like you to meet the Prescott-Beniot family," Jovie said, her pride evident as she made introductions. "Jackie, Lauren, and Melody. This is my daughter Emma."

"The famous daughter we've heard so much about," Lauren said warmly, stepping forward to shake Emma's hand. "It's wonderful to finally meet you."

"Mom's told me incredible things about all of you," Emma replied. "How you've built this amazing community around Charlie Joe's restaurant, how you've made her feel like family again." Her voice carried genuine gratitude. "She's been happier these past few months than I've seen her in years."

Jackie felt touched by the simple acknowledgment. "She's been essential to everything we've accomplished. We're the ones who should be grateful."

Emma examined their competition setup with obvious interest. "This looks professional. Mom always said competition barbecue was different from restaurant cooking, but I never understood how different until now. I was just a kid when she quit and started working for Charlie Joe."

"Want to see how we're managing the temperature control?" Melody offered, gesturing toward their monitoring system. "Your mother's been teaching us precision techniques that require constant attention."

As Melody explained their setup, Jackie noticed how Emma listened with the focused attention of someone who'd learned to appreciate every moment of feeling well enough to engage fully with the world. There was something both fragile and resilient about her that reminded Jackie of spring flowers, delicate but determined to bloom.

"The doctors finally cleared me to be around groups of people again," Emma explained, perhaps sensing Jackie's careful observation. "My immune system is strong enough now to handle exposure to crowds, which means I can finally see Mom in action at the kind of event she used to live for. I remember visiting her. She was strong, in charge, happy."

Jovie smiled at her daughter with pride.

"How are you feeling?" Lauren asked gently.

"Good days and challenging days, but more good days lately," Emma replied with the matter-of-fact tone of someone who'd learned to manage chronic illness with grace. "Good enough to come cheer on Mom's team and finally meet the family she's been raving about."

Jovie wiped her hands on her apron and moved to stand beside her daughter. "Emma's been wanting to visit the restaurant, but we've been waiting for her strength to build up and for the doctors to give full clearance for social activities."

"Well, now that you're here, you get to see Jovie in her element," Jackie said. "She's been coaching us like a drill sergeant, but we're learning techniques we never knew existed."

"That sounds like Mom," Emma said with fond amusement. "She doesn't do anything halfway."

They spent the next twenty minutes showing Emma their competition process, with Jovie explaining techniques while clearly enjoying having her daughter witness her expertise. Jackie watched the interaction with warm appreciation for how illness had clearly strengthened rather than weakened the bond between mother and daughter.

"I should probably head back before the crowds get too thick," Emma said eventually. "But I wanted to tell you all something." She looked around at each of them seriously. "Mom came back to life when she started working for you. She'd been just going through the motions for so long, focused on taking care of me and managing my treatments. But joining your family, being part of something that mattered beyond just survival. It gave her purpose again."

Jackie felt her throat tighten with emotion. "She gave us purpose too. We couldn't have done any of this without her knowledge and dedication."

"I'm glad you found each other," Emma said simply. "Now I better get out of here before Mom starts worrying about germs and crowd exposure."

"I'll walk you to your car," Jovie said immediately, her protective instincts clearly still on high alert despite Emma's improved health.

After they left, Lauren turned to Jackie with tears in her eyes. "That was beautiful. Seeing Jovie with Emma, seeing how much our restaurant family means to both of them."

"It makes me understand Jovie better," Melody observed. "Her precision, her dedication, her careful approach to everything. She's been managing life-and-death situations for years. Competition barbecue probably feels relatively low-pressure in comparison."

When Jovie returned a few minutes later, her professional demeanor had softened slightly.

"Thank you for being so welcoming to Emma," she said quietly. "She's been looking forward to meeting you for months, but we had to wait for the right time medically."

"She's lovely," Jackie said. "And clearly where you get your strength and determination."

"She gets those qualities from herself," Jovie replied firmly. "But I'm grateful she's finally strong enough to see the life we've built here, to understand why this work matters so much to me."

As they returned to their competition preparations, Jackie felt their team bond had deepened in ways that went beyond cooking techniques or winning strategies.

"Excuse me, are you the Prairie Rose team? Um, Charlie Joe's Angels, right?"

Jackie looked up to see a woman in her late thirties approaching their setup with a professional camera and the kind of bright smile that suggested she was used to getting what she wanted. She had perfectly styled blonde hair, designer jeans that had probably never seen actual work, and the aggressive friendliness of someone building a personal brand.

"I'm Cassie Brennan from Hill Country Eats," the woman continued, not waiting for an answer. "I'm documenting the championship for my blog and social media channels. Mind if I get some shots of your setup?"

"Cassie Brennan," Melody repeated, and Jackie could see her accessing the research she'd done on food bloggers. "You have forty-seven thousand followers on Instagram and a James Beard nomination for digital food writing."

"Fifty-two thousand as of this morning, actually," Cassie said with obvious pride. "And I love featuring underdogs and local stories. A family restaurant team competing in their first championship? That's exactly the kind of authentic narrative my audience craves."

She began taking photos without waiting for permission, capturing their modest setup from multiple angles while chattering about "rustic charm" and "grassroots authenticity." Jackie felt uncomfortable with the attention but couldn't think of a polite way to ask her to stop.

"So, what's your angle?" Cassie asked, lowering her camera. "Family bonding through barbecue? Sisters reunited by tragedy? Small town restaurant fights for recognition?"

"We're just here to compete and learn," Lauren said diplomatically.

"Oh, come on," Cassie pressed. "There's always a story. Inherited restaurant, mysterious uncle, federal murder investigation. That's the kind of backstory that makes for viral content."

Jackie felt her protective instincts kick in. "Our family's past isn't material for your blog."

"Everything's material for content creation," Cassie replied with a laugh that sounded forced. "But don't worry, I only write positive pieces about competitors. Well, usually."

The qualifier hung in the air like a subtle threat. Jackie was about to respond when Jovie intervened smoothly.

"Ma'am, we appreciate the interest, but we need to focus on our cooking right now. Maybe you could check back with us after the judging?"

Cassie's smile became more strained. "Of course. I'll just capture a few more atmospheric shots." She continued photographing, but her movements were more aggressive, her comments more pointed about their "amateur setup" and "charming inexperience."

After she moved on to harass another team, Jackie felt unsettled in a way she couldn't quite define.

"That woman has an agenda," she said to Lauren.

"She's building a brand," Lauren replied. "Food blogging is competitive. She needs content that gets engagement."

"At our expense?"

"Hopefully not, but we can't control what she writes. We can only control our barbecue."

The first round of judging arrived faster than Jackie had expected. At exactly 3 PM, volunteers began collecting chicken entries from each team, placing identical white boxes on a long table where the judges waited. Jackie watched their entry disappear into the crowd of submissions, feeling a mixture of pride and anxiety.

The judging took place in a large tent, closed to competitors and spectators. Jackie could see the silhouettes of judges moving between tables, but the actual evaluation process was hidden from view.

"How long does this take?" she asked Jovie.

"About an hour for each category. They taste every entry, score it according to the rubric, and compile results. No discussion between judges until after they've submitted their individual scores."

"And Tex Morrison is the head judge?"

"Yes, Tex is the head judge, plus four certified BBQ judges from around the state. They're all experienced, all trained in the official scoring system," Jovie confirmed.

Jackie looked toward the judging tent, wondering how their chicken was being evaluated. After three weeks of intensive training, she felt confident in their preparation, but competition judging was still a mystery to her. Their first ever competition, first ever entry. The pressure was on, but also a bit of relief having that one done.

"Think we have a chance?" Lauren asked quietly.

"We have a chance not to embarrass ourselves," Jackie replied. "Anything beyond that is bonus."

The afternoon continued with rib and pulled pork submissions, each category bringing fresh waves of anxiety and anticipation. Their timing was good, their temperature control was excellent, and their presentation looked professional. Whatever happened, they'd given their best effort.

As the sun began to set, casting long shadows across the park, the atmosphere grew more tense. Competitors clustered around their setups, trying to look casual while clearly nervous about results. Family members and friends filled the spectator areas, and local media wandered among the teams conducting interviews.

"Final call for brisket entries," announced Martin Delgado, the competition organizer. He was a harried-looking man in his fifties who'd been running around all day with a clipboard and a perpetually worried expression.

Jackie and Lauren carefully arranged their brisket in the regulation box, making sure each piece met the presentation standards Jovie had drilled into them. The brisket had a perfect smoke ring, perfect color, and the moisture level looked spot on.

"This is it," Jackie said as she sealed the box. "Four categories submitted. Whatever happens now is out of our hands."

"The waiting is the worst part," Jovie said. "Competition cooking is hurry up and wait. Intense preparation followed by nothing to do but worry."

As the final entries were collected and delivered to the judging tent, Jackie noticed increased activity around the judges' area. Volunteers were moving more urgently, and she could hear raised voices from inside the tent.

She also noticed Wade Brooks having what appeared to be an intense conversation with Martin Delgado near the judging tent. Wade's body language was aggressive, and Delgado looked uncomfortable. The conversation ended abruptly when Wade noticed Jackie watching, and he stalked back toward his team's area.

"That didn't look friendly," Lauren observed.

"Wade's probably complaining about something," Jovie said. "He always has grievances about judging procedures, entry requirements, volunteer assignments. Charlie Joe used to say Wade could find fault with a perfect sunset."

Martin went into the large tent while Wade moved back to his team, giving a look at Jackie and Lauren.

"If looks could kill," Jackie said with a chuckle.

Martin Delgado emerged from the tent looking pale and shaken. He conferred briefly with several officials, then walked quickly toward a large RV parked behind the judging area. Jackie recognized it as Tex Morrison's, the legendary pitmaster who always traveled with his custom setup for out-of-town competitions.

"Something's wrong," Melody observed, pointing toward the tent where several people had gathered in what looked like an urgent conference.

Minutes later, the sound of sirens filled the evening air. An ambulance, followed by Sheriff Martinez's patrol car, raced into the park with lights flashing. Emergency personnel disappeared into Tex's RV while shocked competitors and spectators gathered at a respectable distance.

Jackie felt her stomach drop as she realized something terrible had happened.

"Is that...?" Lauren began, but her question was answered when Sheriff Martinez emerged from the RV and began speaking urgently into his radio. His expression was grim, professional, and deeply troubled.

Martin Delgado approached the microphone that had been set up for the awards ceremony, his hands shaking as he adjusted the height.

"Ladies and gentlemen, competitors and spectators," he began, his voice barely steady. "I regret to inform you that Judge Tex Morrison has been found deceased in his RV. The circumstances are currently under investigation."

A shocked silence fell over the park, broken only by the sound of emergency radio chatter and someone crying in the distance.

"The competition is suspended pending investigation," Martin continued. "Please remain in the park until authorities have had a chance to speak with you. We ask for your patience and cooperation during this difficult time."

Jackie felt Lauren grab her arm as the full implications hit her. Tex Morrison, the legendary pitmaster who had encouraged them just days before, was dead. And given Sheriff Martinez's presence and the serious expressions on the emergency personnel's faces, it wasn't looking like natural causes.

"Food poisoning," someone near them whispered. "Had to be food poisoning. He was judging barbecue all afternoon."

"But which team?" another voice asked. "Whose food killed him?"

Jackie looked around the park at the dozens of teams, each of whom had submitted food that Tex Morrison had tasted just hours before. If he'd died from food poisoning, every single competitor was now a potential suspect.

Including them.

"Mom," Melody said quietly, "we need to secure our equipment and ingredients. If this becomes a criminal investigation, they'll want to test everything."

Jackie was struck by her niece's practical thinking even in the midst of shock and grief. Melody was right. If Tex had died from contaminated food, every team's setup would become potential evidence.

As Sheriff Martinez began organizing his response and additional law enforcement vehicles arrived at the park, Jackie realized their first barbecue competition had just become something much more serious and dangerous.

Their next challenge wouldn't be impressing judges with their brisket. It would be proving they hadn't accidentally killed a legend.

Chapter Four

Sheriff Ray Martinez had transformed from Lauren's gentle suitor into a focused law enforcement professional in the span of twenty minutes. Jackie watched him move methodically through the park, organizing his deputies, securing the crime scene, and establishing interview protocols with the efficiency of someone who'd handled serious investigations before.

"I need all competitors to remain at their cooking stations," he announced through a bullhorn. "Do not touch your equipment or dispose of any ingredients until we've had a chance to document everything. This is now a potential crime scene."

Potential crime scene. The words sent a chill through Jackie that had nothing to do with the evening breeze. If Tex Morrison's death was being treated as a crime rather than an accident, every person in the park was now a suspect.

"Deputies will be conducting brief interviews with each team," Martinez continued. "We appreciate your cooperation and patience. The sooner we can gather preliminary information; the sooner we can determine next steps."

Jackie noticed how carefully he'd phrased that. *Preliminary information* and *determine next steps* rather than *solve the murder* or *find the killer.* He was being professionally cautious, but the implication was clear. Someone in the park might have killed Tex Morrison.

"We might need to retain a lawyer," Jackie said matter-of-factly.

Lauren turned to Jackie with obvious frustration. "I can't believe you're even considering getting a lawyer. That makes us look guilty."

"It makes us look prudent," Jackie shot back, her legal training evident in her tone. "Lauren, we submitted food that a judge tasted before he died. We're not just witnesses. We're potential suspects whether we like it or not."

"Ray wouldn't treat us like suspects. He knows us."

"Ray is a professional law enforcement officer investigating a murder. Personal feelings don't change legal procedures. I should know. I've been in that position." Jackie's voice carried the patience of someone explaining basic concepts to a child, which clearly irritated Lauren.

"Don't talk to me like I'm naive, Jackie. I may not have a law degree, but I understand that calling a lawyer when we haven't been charged with anything sends the wrong message to everyone."

"And I understand that failing to protect ourselves legally could destroy everything we've built here if this investigation goes sideways." Jackie's tone grew sharper. "You're thinking with your heart instead of your head."

"And you're thinking like a lawyer instead of a sister," Lauren replied, her cheeks flushing with anger. "We're innocent, Jackie. We have nothing to hide, and acting like we do will hurt our reputation in this community."

"Our reputation won't matter if we're in prison for murder."

"That's ridiculous! You know we didn't kill anyone."

"What I know and what I can prove in court are two different things," Jackie said firmly. "Lauren, I've seen innocent people get convicted because they were too trusting of the system."

Melody looked up from her notebook, clearly uncomfortable with the rising tension between her mother and aunt. "Maybe we could compromise? Consult with Harold Westin informally but don't retain him officially unless circumstances change?"

Both sisters looked at her, then at each other, the anger in their faces softening slightly as they realized they had fallen back into their old habit of arguing and it was frightening Melody.

"That's... actually a reasonable approach," Jackie admitted reluctantly.

"Fine," Lauren said, though her tone remained stiff. "But I still think you're overreacting."

"And I think you're being dangerously naive," Jackie replied. "But we'll do it Melody's way."

"Team Charlie Joe's Angels?" A young deputy approached their station, notebook in hand. "Sheriff Martinez would like to speak with you now."

Jackie and Lauren exchanged a smile at the sound of their team's name. A bit of comic relief in the middle of a tragedy. The young deputy missed the joke.

They found Martinez in the park's administrative building, which had been converted into a temporary interview facility. He'd set up in the main conference room, and Jackie could see other deputies taking statements from competitors in smaller offices throughout the building.

"Ladies," Martinez said, standing when they entered. His tone was professionally neutral, but Jackie caught the brief look of concern that passed between him and Lauren. "I need to ask you some questions about your interactions with Judge Morrison today."

"Of course," Jackie replied. "We want to help however we can."

"When did you last see Mr. Morrison alive?"

"Just before 2 PM," Lauren said. "He stopped by our station to wish us luck and compliment our setup."

"Did he appear ill or distressed at that time?"

"Not at all," Jackie said. "He seemed energetic, enthusiastic about the competition. He was making his rounds, talking to different teams."

Martinez made notes as they spoke, his professional demeanor never slipping despite his obvious familiarity with their family. "Did Mr. Morrison taste any of your food during that visit?"

"No," Melody said immediately. "Judges aren't allowed to sample from cooking stations during the competition. He mentioned that specifically. He said he was looking forward to tasting our entries during official judging."

"And what entries did you submit?"

Jovie provided the timeline: chicken at 3 PM, ribs at 4 PM, pulled pork at 5 PM, brisket at 6 PM. All within regulation boxes, all submitted through proper channels, all handled by volunteers who transported entries from teams to judges.

"Did you notice anything unusual about the judging process?" Martinez asked. "Any delays, disruptions, irregularities?"

"The judging seemed to run on schedule," Lauren said. "We could see activity in the tent, but of course we couldn't observe the actual tasting."

"When did you first realize something was wrong?"

"When you arrived," Jackie said. "We saw the ambulance, then you emerging from Mr. Morrison's RV looking... well, like you'd discovered something serious."

Martinez nodded grimly. "What can you tell me about your interactions with other competitors today?"

Jackie thought carefully before responding. "Most teams kept to themselves, focused on their cooking. A few friendly conversations, but nothing that seemed significant."

"What about Cassie Brennan, the food blogger?"

"She interviewed us briefly this morning," Lauren said. "Took some photos, asked about our story. She seemed... intense about getting content for her blog."

"Intense how?"

"Pushy," Jackie said bluntly. "She kept probing for personal details, family drama, anything that would make for what she called 'viral content.' When we declined to discuss our uncle's murder case, she got a bit aggressive."

Martinez's attention sharpened. "Aggressive in what way?"

"She made comments about our 'amateur setup' and 'charming inexperience,'" Melody recounted precisely.

"Her tone suggested she wasn't pleased that we weren't providing the narrative she wanted," Jovie added.

"Did she mention having any history with Judge Morrison?"

The women exchanged glances. "Not directly," Jackie said. "But she did mention only writing positive pieces about competitors, 'usually.' The way she said it suggested there might be exceptions."

Martinez made additional notes, then looked up at them with an expression that mixed his personal concern with professional necessity. "I need to ask this directly. Did any of you have any reason to want harm to come to Tex Morrison?"

"Absolutely not," Jackie said immediately. "He was encouraging, supportive, exactly what you'd want from a judge. He visited our restaurant a few weeks ago and was completely gracious."

"He even complimented our food and gave us constructive advice," Lauren added. "If anything, we were hoping to impress him with our competition entries."

"And your opinion of him as a judge?"

"Legendary," Jovie said. "Tex Morrison was respected throughout the barbecue community. Fair, knowledgeable, impossible to bribe or influence. If he scored your food poorly, you knew you deserved it. If he scored it well, you knew you'd earned it."

Martinez finished his notes and closed his notebook. "That's all for now. I may need to speak with you again as the investigation develops, but for now you are free to leave."

As they began to stand, Martinez cleared his throat. "Lauren, could I speak with you privately for a moment?"

Jackie caught the look that passed between them and made a quick decision. "We'll wait by the car," she said diplomatically.

After Jackie, Jovie, and Melody left the conference room, Martinez's professional demeanor softened noticeably. He moved around the desk to sit in the chair beside Lauren rather than across from her, the physical proximity changing the dynamic from official to personal.

"How are you really handling this?" he asked, his voice gentle with concern. "I know being questioned in a murder investigation can't be easy, especially when you're innocent."

Lauren felt warmth spread through her chest at his obvious care for her well-being. "I keep thinking about what could have happened if we'd been the ones to submit the food that killed him. The guilt would be unbearable, even if it was an accident."

"But you didn't, and it wasn't an accident," Ray said firmly. "Someone deliberately poisoned Tex Morrison, and I'm going to find out who."

"What if they don't get caught? What if whoever did this decides we know too much or pose some kind of threat?"

Ray leaned closer, his brown eyes serious and reassuring. "Lauren, I will protect you and your family. But I also want to assure you that this investigation won't compromise what's been developing between us. I'll maintain complete professional objectivity during the case, but that doesn't change how I feel about you personally."

"How do you feel about me personally?" Lauren asked, surprised by her own boldness.

"I think you're one of the strongest, most genuine people I've ever met. I think you've built something beautiful with your family and your restaurant. And I like where we have been going with this the past several months, even though both of our schedules leave little time for us. I won't let this investigation get in the way of that either."

Lauren felt her cheeks warm with pleasure and relief. She'd been worried that the investigation would end whatever had been beginning between them, that being questioned as a potential suspect would make her too complicated for him to pursue.

"I'd like that too," she said softly.

"Good." Ray stood up, his professional demeanor returning as voices approached the conference room. "In the meantime, I need you to be very careful. Until we catch Tex's killer, everyone connected to this competition could potentially be at risk."

"At risk how?"

"If someone killed to protect a secret, they might kill again to keep that secret safe. Don't investigate on your own, don't take unnecessary chances, and if anything feels wrong or dangerous, call me immediately."

As she rejoined the others outside the administrative building, Lauren felt both comforted by Ray's personal concern and sobered by his professional warnings. The investigation had the potential to bring them closer together, but it also carried real dangers that could threaten everything they'd built.

"Everything okay?" Jackie asked, noting Lauren's thoughtful expression.

"Ray wanted to make sure I understood how serious this investigation might become," Lauren said, which was true without revealing the personal aspects of their conversation.

As they left the administrative building, Lauren found herself looking back to see Ray coordinating with his deputies, his tall figure moving with quiet authority as he managed the complex investigation. The thought that she might have found someone who appreciated both her strength and her vulnerabilities, who could separate professional duty from personal feelings, filled her with a hope she hadn't felt in years.

She allowed herself to imagine what it might be like to have someone in her life who understood the balance between duty and care, between professional responsibility and personal connection.

But first, they had to survive whatever dangers Tex Morrison's murder had unleashed. And despite Ray's reassurances about professional objectivity, Lauren knew that being emotionally involved with a potential suspect's family member would complicate his investigation in ways neither of them could fully predict.

As the park slowly emptied and teams were released after questioning, Jackie realized their barbecue competition had become something much more dangerous. Someone had used the event to commit murder, and until that person was caught, everyone who'd participated would remain under suspicion.

Including them.

The thought that someone could use their beloved barbecue, the food that brought communities together, that represented hospitality and tradition, as a weapon for murder made Jackie angrier than she'd been in months.

Whoever had killed Tex Morrison had violated something sacred. And Jackie was determined to help bring them to justice, even if it meant conducting their own investigation alongside Sheriff Martinez's official one.

Chapter Five

By the time they returned to the restaurant that evening, Jackie felt like she'd aged ten years in one day. The competition equipment sat unused in their truck, a reminder of how quickly their exciting challenge had turned into a nightmare. She couldn't shake the image of Sheriff Martinez's grim expression or the weight of being questioned as potential suspects in a murder investigation.

"I can't believe Tex is dead," Lauren said, slumping into one of the restaurant chairs. "He was so alive, so passionate about barbecue. Who would want to kill him?"

"Someone with a serious grudge," Jackie replied, her legal mind already working through possibilities. "Food poisoning could be accidental, but Ray said there were irregularities. That suggests deliberate poisoning disguised to look like food contamination."

Melody had spread her competition notes across a table and was adding new observations about the day's events. "The killer would need specific knowledge of competition procedures," she said. "They'd have to know how the judging worked, when entries were submitted, how to ensure Tex would taste their contaminated food."

"Which means it's probably someone familiar with barbecue competitions," Jackie added. "Not a random outsider."

"Or someone who did their research," Lauren pointed out. "Competition rules are public information. Anyone could learn the procedures."

Jackie stood and began pacing, a habit from her lawyer days when she was working through complex cases. "Let's think about this systematically. Who had motive to kill Tex Morrison?"

"Smoke Jackson seemed pretty angry during the questioning," Lauren said. "And that other competitor mentioned something about Tex costing him a championship."

"Smoke's the obvious suspect," Jackie agreed. "Which could mean he's guilty, or it could mean the real killer wanted him to look guilty. What do we know about his history with Tex?"

Melody consulted her notebook. "According to my research, Billy 'Smoke' Jackson placed second in the East Texas Regional Championship three years ago. Tex Morrison was the head judge.

Smoke's brisket scored perfectly in taste and tenderness, but Tex gave him low marks for appearance, claiming the presentation was sloppy."

"That cost him the championship?" Lauren asked.

"First place came with a ten-thousand-dollar prize and sponsorship opportunities that could have launched Smoke's barbecue business," Melody explained. "Instead, he's still competing at regional events and struggling financially."

"That's serious motive," Jackie said. "Public humiliation, financial loss, career damage. But would he really wait three years to get revenge?"

"Maybe something else happened more recently," Lauren suggested. "Maybe Tex did something else that pushed Smoke over the edge."

Jackie felt the familiar thrill of investigation, the intellectual challenge of piecing together facts and motives. "We need more information about all the potential suspects. Who else had access to the judging process?"

"Cassie Brennan," Melody said immediately. "She was photographing everything, talking to everyone. She could have learned details about competition procedures."

"And she definitely had an attitude about something," Lauren added. "That comment about usually writing positive pieces suggested she'd written negative reviews before."

"Food bloggers have real power these days," Jackie mused. "A bad review from someone with fifty thousand followers could destroy a restaurant or end a pitmaster's career. What if Tex had given her barbecue joint a terrible review?"

"We should find out if she owns a restaurant," Melody said, making a note. "Also, whether Tex has reviewed any establishments recently."

"What about Martin Delgado, the competition organizer?" Lauren asked. "He seemed really nervous all day, even before Tex died."

Jackie had noticed that too. Martin had been constantly checking his clipboard, consulting with officials, looking generally stressed about more than normal event management issues.

"Competition organizers handle significant money," Jackie said. "Entry fees, prize funds, vendor payments. If there was financial irregularity, Tex would be in a position to notice as head judge."

"What about Wade Brooks?" Melody asked, looking up from her notes. "I observed several concerning interactions between him and the competition officials."

"Wade Brooks was the one arguing with Martin just before Tex was found, right?" Jackie asked.

"Yes, owns Brooks' Barbecue Barn from Cedar Hill," Lauren explained.

"Yes, I do remember him," Jackie said slowly. "He was watching our setup pretty intently during the morning prep. Not in a friendly, competitive way. More like he was looking for problems."

Melody flipped through her systematic notes from the day. "Wade Brooks had multiple interactions with Martin Delgado throughout the competition. At 10:30 AM, they had what appeared to be a heated discussion near the judging tent. At 2:15 PM, Brooks approached the volunteer check-in area and seemed to be questioning procedures. At 4:45 PM, shortly before Tex Morrison collapsed, when we observed Brooks having another intense conversation with Delgado."

"That's a lot of official contact for a regular competitor," Jackie observed.

"Plus, Wade seemed to know Tex personally," Lauren added. "When they announced Tex as head judge this morning, I saw Wade's expression change. He looked... angry. Like seeing Tex there ruined his day."

Jackie felt her investigative instincts sharpening. "Personal animosity with the head judge, multiple confrontations with the organizer, unusual interest in competition procedures. That's a pattern of behavior worth examining."

"There's something else," Melody said, consulting her timeline notes. "Wade Brooks was absent from his cooking station during the critical period when ribs entries were being submitted to judges. His team members were handling the preparation while he was elsewhere."

"Where was he?" Lauren asked.

"Unknown. I noted his absence at 4:20 PM and didn't observe his return until that fight with Martin Delgado, approximately five minutes before Tex Morrison's medical emergency began."

Jackie stopped pacing and looked at her niece with admiration. Melody's systematic documentation was proving invaluable for their investigation.

"So, Wade Brooks had opportunity. He was unaccounted for during the critical time period. He had apparent personal issues with Tex Morrison. And he was confrontational with officials throughout the day," Jackie summarized.

"And as a restaurant owner, he'd understand food safety protocols well enough to know how to circumvent them," Lauren added.

Melody made additional notes in her precise handwriting. "Wade Brooks appears to meet all criteria for a viable suspect: motive, means, opportunity, and local knowledge necessary for the murder method."

"But what would his specific motive be?" Lauren asked. "Professional jealousy? Business competition?"

"We need to find out more about his history with Tex," Jackie said. "Personal grievances, professional conflicts, anything that might have escalated to murder."

"His restaurant is only fifteen miles away," Melody observed. "We could visit Brooks' Barbecue Barn and assess his operation, maybe engage him in conversation about his competition experiences."

Jackie felt both excitement and apprehension at the suggestion. Direct investigation could provide valuable information, but it would also put them in potential danger if Wade Brooks was indeed their killer.

"That might be worth doing," Jackie said carefully. "But we'd need to be subtle about it. Just a casual visit to try the food, maybe some general conversation about barbecue competition."

"We need to be careful," Lauren said suddenly. "If we start asking too many questions, people might think we're trying to deflect suspicion from ourselves."

"Or they might think we're concerned citizens trying to help find the truth," Jackie countered. "We knew Tex, we respected him, and we want his killer caught. That's not suspicious, that's decent."

"Plus," Melody added pragmatically, "we're already suspects. Conducting our own investigation won't make us more suspicious, and it might help us discover information that clears us."

Jackie made a decision. "We investigate, but we do it smart. We use our individual strengths, and we share everything we learn with each other and with Sheriff Martinez when appropriate."

"What are our strengths?" Lauren asked.

"You're good with people," Jackie said. "You can talk to the other competitors, get them to open up about what they observed or heard. People trust you in ways they don't trust lawyers or cops."

"I can analyze patterns and inconsistencies in testimony," Melody added. "Also, research backgrounds, financial records, competition histories."

"And I can think like a prosecutor," Jackie said. "Build cases, evaluate evidence, understand legal procedures that might affect the investigation."

"Where do we start?" Lauren asked.

Jackie consulted her watch. It was nearly 10 PM, too late for most approaches, but not too late for research. "Tonight, we research. Melody, dig into the backgrounds of everyone we met today. Look for connections to Tex, reasons for conflict, anything that seems unusual."

"I can access competition records, social media profiles, business registrations," Melody confirmed. "Also, news articles, review sites, legal filings."

"Lauren, think about the conversations you had today. Who seemed nervous, who asked unusual questions, who knew more than they should have about competition procedures or about Tex personally?"

"I talked to maybe a dozen people during setup and cooking," Lauren said. "I'll write down everything I can remember about each conversation."

"And I'll review what we know about the actual poisoning method," Jackie said. "Ray mentioned irregularities that suggested deliberate contamination. I want to understand how someone could have guaranteed that Tex would consume the poison."

They worked in companionable silence for the next hour. Each focused on their assigned research. Jackie found herself thinking about Uncle Charlie Joe's investigation methods. He'd been methodical, patient, focused on documentation rather than dramatic confrontations. Those same approaches could work for solving Tex Morrison's murder.

"Found something," Melody announced, looking up from her laptop. "Cassie Brennan owns a barbecue restaurant in Austin called Grillin' Dreams. It opened eighteen months ago with significant social media fanfare."

"Any connection to Tex Morrison?" Jackie asked.

"Yes. Six months after opening, Tex Morrison reviewed Grillin' Dreams for Texas BBQ Monthly. The review was... not positive."

Melody turned on her laptop so they could read the review. Tex's critique was thorough and devastating: overcooked brisket, under seasoned ribs, inconsistent temperature control, poor presentation, and what he called 'Instagram-friendly appearance masking fundamental technique failures.'

"Ouch," Lauren said. "That would hurt."

"It did more than hurt," Melody continued. "According to online reviews, Grillin' Dreams saw a significant decline in customers after Tex's review was published. Several food blogs referenced his critique when writing their own negative reviews."

"How significant a decline?" Jackie asked.

"Based on social media activity and review patterns, probably thirty to forty percent reduction in business. For a new restaurant, that could be fatal."

Jackie felt pieces clicking into place. "So, Cassie had both professional and personal reasons to resent Tex Morrison. His review threatened her business and her credibility as a food expert."

"Plus, she was here today with full access to the competition area," Lauren added. "She was photographing everything, talking to everyone, moving around freely."

"We need to find out more about her movements today," Jackie said. "Did anyone see her near the judging tent? Did she have opportunity to contaminate food entries?"

"I'll check if there are photos from today's event posted online," Melody said. "Social media posts might show her location at various times."

"What about Smoke Jackson?" Lauren asked. "Did you find anything about recent interactions with Tex?"

Melody scrolled through her notes. "Smoke's been struggling financially. His barbecue catering business has been losing contracts to newer competitors. He's also been vocal on social media about judging inconsistency and favoritism in competitions."

"Vocal how?" Jackie asked.

"Several posts in the past year complaining about judges who favor 'trendy techniques over traditional methods' and 'social media darlings over serious pitmasters.' He never mentioned Tex by name, but the timing suggests he might have been referring to recent judging decisions Tex was involved in."

"So, Smoke had ongoing resentment, not just the three-year-old championship loss," Jackie concluded. "Current financial pressure plus long-term grudge equals strong motive."

"But he's also the obvious suspect," Lauren pointed out. "If Smoke wanted to kill Tex, would he really do it at a public competition where he'd be the first-person investigators looked at?"

"Desperate people don't always think clearly," Jackie said. "Or maybe he thought the food poisoning would look accidental and he wouldn't be suspected at all."

"We should also consider Wade Brooks," Melody said, consulting her notes. "I observed him near the judging area multiple times throughout the day, including that heated conversation with Martin Delgado shortly before Tex Morrison collapsed."

"Wade definitely had issues with Tex," Lauren added. "Jovie told me that last year at the Fredericksburg competition, Wade accused Tex of having 'city biases' against traditional rural pitmasters. Said judges like Tex were ruining barbecue culture by favoring 'fancy techniques over honest cooking.'"

"That's a pretty specific grudge," Jackie said. "And Wade would know enough about barbecue operations to understand how to contaminate food without being obvious about it."

They continued researching until nearly midnight, building profiles of potential suspects and mapping out what they knew about the day's events. By the time they finished, Jackie felt like they had a solid foundation for investigation, but also a clear sense of how much they still didn't know.

"Tomorrow," she said as they prepared to close up, "we start talking to people. Lauren, see if you can connect with some of the other competitors who are still in town. Find out what they observed about Tex's behavior, who he talked to, whether he seemed concerned about anything."

"I can call some of the teams whose contact information I got today," Lauren agreed. "Most of them are staying in local motels tonight before driving home tomorrow or the next day."

"Melody, keep digging into backgrounds, but also start mapping timeline and opportunity. Who was where when entries were submitted? Who had access to the judging area? Who could have contaminated food without being observed?"

"I'll create a visual timeline with location tracking for all major players," Melody said. "That should help identify windows of opportunity."

As they locked up the restaurant and moved up to their apartment, Jackie felt both determined and apprehensive about what they were undertaking. They were essentially conducting a parallel investigation to Sheriff Martinez's official inquiry, which could either help catch the killer or land them in serious trouble.

But Tex Morrison had been kind to them, encouraging about their competition efforts, and generous with his expertise. He'd deserved better than dying alone in his RV from deliberate poisoning. If they could help find his killer, they owed it to him to try.

"One more thing," Jackie said. "We don't investigate alone. If we meet with potential suspects or go anywhere that could be dangerous, we go together. The person who killed Tex has already shown they're willing to commit murder. We don't give them the opportunity to try it again."

"Agreed," Lauren said immediately.

"Statistically, serial killers are rare," Melody observed. "The probability that Tex's murderer would kill again is relatively low."

"Tell that to Uncle Charlie Joe," Jackie replied grimly. "His killer turned out to be part of a criminal organization responsible for multiple deaths over decades. We don't take chances."

As she settled in for the night, Jackie found herself thinking about patterns and probabilities. Melody was right that most murders were isolated incidents, but their family had already been touched by one case involving systematic killing.

She hoped Tex Morrison's death was a simple case of personal revenge or professional rivalry. But her instincts, honed by both legal experience and recent family history, suggested they should prepare for the possibility that the truth was more complicated than anyone realized.

The barbecue competition was supposed to be their biggest challenge. Solving a murder was definitely not what they'd signed up for.

Chapter Six

The fifteen-mile drive to Cedar Hill gave Jackie time to second-guess their decision to investigate Wade Brooks directly. Unlike their careful background research on Smoke Jackson and Cassie Brennan, visiting Wade's restaurant would put them in direct contact with a potential murder suspect.

"Maybe we should have told Sheriff Martinez what we were planning," Lauren said, echoing Jackie's concerns as they pulled into the gravel parking lot of Brooks' Barbecue Barn.

"We're just having lunch," Jackie replied, though her lawyer instincts were warning her they were walking into potentially dangerous territory. "Three restaurant owners trying the competition. Nothing suspicious about that."

Melody looked up from the notebook where she'd been reviewing her competition observations during the drive. "I've prepared a list of casual conversation topics that might elicit relevant information without appearing investigative," she said. "Questions about his competition history, local barbecue community relationships, and general opinions about judging standards."

"Smart. Keep it handy, just in case," Jackie said before climbing out of her car.

The building that housed Brooks' Barbecue Barn looked like it had started life as a roadside diner in the 1960s and had been modified multiple times since then. A hand-painted sign advertised "AUTHENTIC TEXAS BBQ SINCE 1999" in faded red letters, and smoke drifted from a collection of mismatched smokers behind the building.

The interior had the worn-but-clean aesthetic of a place that had seen better days. Red vinyl booths lined the walls, their surfaces cracked from years of use, and the smell of hickory smoke mixed with industrial cleaning solution. Hunting trophies and local high school sports photos covered every available wall space, creating a dense collage of small town pride and rural masculinity.

Wade Brooks looked up from behind the counter when they entered, and Jackie saw recognition flicker across his features before settling into barely concealed hostility.

"Well, if it isn't the Prairie Rose competition team. What was your cutesy name, Charlie Joe's Angels or something?" he asked with the kind of aggressive joviality that fooled no one. "Come to scope out the real barbecue before your next amateur attempt?"

Jackie forced a pleasant smile. "Just wanted to try your food. We heard good things about your brisket."

Melody immediately began her systematic assessment, her eyes taking in the restaurant's layout, customer count, and operational details with the kind of focused attention that most people wouldn't notice.

"Twenty-three years of perfecting my technique," Wade said, his chest puffing with obvious pride. "Not like some people who inherit a restaurant and think they can just waltz into competition barbecue."

The comment carried enough venom that Lauren instinctively stepped closer to Jackie. Wade Brooks was a big man, probably six-two and well over two hundred and fifty pounds, with the kind of bulk that suggested he'd been physically imposing his entire life. His graying beard was neatly trimmed, but his eyes held the hard edge of someone who felt the world owed him more than it had delivered.

"What can I get you ladies?" he asked, making the word 'ladies' sound like an insult.

"Three brisket plates," Jackie said. "And maybe some of those burnt ends if you have them."

"Oh, I've got burnt ends," Wade replied. "Real ones, not the fancy cubed nonsense some places try to pass off. My daddy taught me to make burnt ends the right way, back when Kansas City pitmasters still had respect for tradition."

Jackie wanted to counter with this is Texas but bit her tongue. They were supposed to at least appear friendly.

As Wade moved to prepare their order, Melody discreetly consulted her notebook and began making quiet observations to Jackie and Lauren.

"Restaurant occupancy approximately fifteen percent during peak lunch hours," she murmured. "Minimal staff which appears to be Wade plus one kitchen assistant. Equipment visible through service window includes one primary smoker, standard commercial kitchen setup. Financial indicators suggest declining business volume."

Jackie noticed the restaurant was nearly empty despite being lunch time. Only two other tables were occupied. One by an elderly couple sharing a plate of ribs, the other by a man in work clothes who looked like a regular customer.

The contrast with their bustling lunch crowds at Charlie Joe's was stark, and Jackie began to understand why Wade might harbor such resentment toward their success.

"You know," Wade called from behind the counter where he was slicing brisket with more force than necessary, "Charlie Joe used to come in here back in the early days. Before he got too big for his britches."

"Really?" Lauren asked, settling into a booth near the window.

"Oh yes. Back when he was still learning, still humble about the craft. We used to trade techniques, share suppliers, help each other out during busy weekends." Wade's voice carried genuine nostalgia mixed with bitterness. "Course, that all changed once his place got written up in those magazines."

Jackie watched Wade's movements carefully as he prepared their plates. His knife work was efficient and skilled, demonstrating the kind of precision that came from decades of practice. It also demonstrated exactly the kind of knowledge about food preparation that could be useful for someone planning to poison a meal.

"Charlie Joe always spoke highly of you," Jackie said diplomatically, though she wasn't sure if it was true.

Wade snorted. "Charlie Joe spoke highly of anyone who might be useful to him. Once he decided he was building some kind of barbecue empire, old friendships didn't matter much."

"Empire?" Lauren asked.

"All those expansions, the catering business, the weekend events. Charlie Joe went from being a local pitmaster to trying to be some kind of Hill Country barbecue mogul." Wade brought their plates to the table with unnecessary force, the ceramic clattering against the laminate surface. "Man forgot where he came from."

As far as Jackie knew, there weren't any expansions until they arrived and did them. He had only done small catering jobs for the church and library, things like that. The weekend events, she had to assume, were his Sunday community meals.

But again, she wanted to appear friendly, so she focused on eating her meal instead of pointing out the inconsistencies in his story.

The food was actually quite good, Jackie had to admit. The brisket had a proper smoke ring and the kind of tender consistency that came from careful temperature control. The sauce was tangy without being overpowering, and the burnt ends had the perfect balance of crispy exterior and juicy interior.

"This is excellent," Lauren said honestly.

"The preparation demonstrates significant technical skill," Melody added, studying her plate with analytical precision. "Consistent moisture retention, appropriate smoke penetration, balanced seasoning ratios."

Wade's expression softened slightly at the compliments. "Like I said, twenty-three years of getting it right. I don't need fancy equipment or trendy techniques. Just good meat, good smoke, and the patience to do it properly."

"Speaking of technique," Jackie said carefully, "we're still learning about competition judging standards. Was Tex Morrison someone who appreciated traditional approaches?"

The change in Wade's demeanor was immediate and dramatic. His face flushed red, and his hands clenched into fists on the table.

Melody immediately began documenting the behavioral shift, her pen moving across her notebook in small, precise movements that looked like casual notetaking but were actually systematic observation records.

"Tex Morrison," Wade spat the name like it tasted bad. "That man was everything wrong with modern barbecue judging. More concerned with presentation than flavor, more interested in innovation than tradition."

"Subject displays elevated stress response to Morrison's name," Melody murmured quietly to Lauren, but Wade narrowed his eyes as if he heard her. "Increased vocal tension, clenched fists, facial flushing. Physical manifestation of strong negative emotional association."

"You sound like you had some personal experience with his judging," Lauren observed.

"Three competitions," Wade said bitterly. "Three times I should have placed in the top five, three times Tex Morrison scored me low because my technique was 'outdated' and my presentation was 'unrefined.'" He made air quotes around the words, his voice dripping with sarcasm.

"That must have been frustrating," Jackie said.

"Frustrating? It was criminal. That man cost me thousands of dollars in prize money and sponsorship opportunities because he had some kind of bias against pitmasters who learned their craft the traditional way."

Wade was leaning forward now, his voice rising with emotion. The elderly couple at the other table glanced over nervously, and the man in work clothes was openly staring.

"Last year at Fredericksburg, I had the best brisket I'd ever cooked. Perfect bark, perfect tenderness, flavor that would make you weep. You know what score Tex gave me? Seventy-three out of a hundred. Said my 'presentation lacked creativity' and my 'flavor profile was one-dimensional.'"

"One-dimensional," Lauren repeated, while Melody continued her discrete documentation.

"Statistical analysis of competition scoring suggests that a seventy-three represents bottom quartile performance," Melody observed matter-of-factly. "That would significantly impact overall placement and potential prize earnings."

"One-dimensional! Twenty-three years of perfecting a recipe my grandfather passed down to me, and some city-boy judge calls it one-dimensional because I don't put fancy garnishes on the plate or drizzle sauce in decorative patterns."

Jackie felt a chill as she listened to Wade's increasingly heated rant. The level of personal animosity toward Tex Morrison was far beyond professional disappointment. This was the kind of deep, festering resentment that could drive someone to extreme actions.

Wade sat back in his chair, seeming to realize he'd been talking more than intended. "Anyway, it doesn't matter now, does it? Tex got what was coming to him, and Charlie Joe's gone. Just leaves the rest of us to carry on the traditional way of doing things."

The casual callousness of that statement "Tex got what was coming to him" sent ice through Jackie's veins. It was exactly the kind of comment someone might make if they felt justified in taking revenge.

Melody's pen paused on her notebook, and Jackie could see her processing the implications of Wade's words with the same systematic precision she applied to everything else.

"What do you mean, 'got what was coming to him?'" Lauren asked carefully.

Wade's eyes sharpened, as if he suddenly remembered he was talking to potential competitors rather than sympathetic listeners. "I mean karma caught up with him. Man spent years destroying other people's dreams and reputations. Bound to catch up eventually."

"Temporal sequence suggests premeditation," Melody murmured, so quietly only Jackie and Lauren could hear. "Subject expresses satisfaction with victim's death, implies justification through 'karma' concept."

"But he died from food poisoning," Jackie pointed out. "That's hardly karma, right? That's just tragic."

"Is it though?" Wade asked, his tone becoming darker. "Man made a career out of criticizing other people's food preparation and safety standards. Maybe he finally encountered some food that wasn't prepared to his *exacting* specifications."

The implication was clear, and Jackie felt her lawyer instincts screaming warnings about continuing this conversation. Wade Brooks wasn't just a disgruntled competitor, he was someone who seemed to feel Tex Morrison's death was justified revenge.

"Well," Jackie said, standing up and placing more than enough money on the table to cover the bill, "thank you for lunch. The food really was excellent."

"You're welcome," Wade replied, though his tone remained cold. "And ladies? Next time you decide to compete, remember that some of us have been doing this longer than you've been thinking about it. Experience counts for something in this business."

As they walked to their car, Jackie felt Wade's eyes following them through the restaurant's front window. The sensation was distinctly unpleasant, like being watched by a predator deciding whether they were worth pursuing.

"Well, that was unsettling," Lauren said once they were safely in the car with doors locked.

"That was a textbook demonstration of barely contained hostility with clear motivational indicators for violent behavior," Melody said, consulting her notebook. "Wade Brooks exhibited multiple red flag behaviors: disproportionate emotional response to victim's name, explicit satisfaction with victim's death, implied justification for violence, and escalating agitation during discussion."

"That was terrifying," Jackie corrected. "Wade Brooks has serious resentment towards Tex Morrison, detailed knowledge of food preparation, and the kind of personality that might justify murder as 'karma.'"

"Plus, he clearly knew both Uncle Charlie Joe and Tex personally," Lauren added. "He would have understood their routines, their relationships, their vulnerabilities."

As they drove back toward Prairie Rose, Jackie's mind was racing through the implications of what they'd learned. Wade Brooks had motive, means, and opportunity, and the kind of bitter personality that could rationalize murder as justified revenge.

"Do we call Sheriff Martinez now?" Lauren asked.

"We need to compile our evidence systematically first," Melody said, already organizing her notes. "I documented seventeen distinct behavioral indicators suggesting guilt or deception, multiple statements expressing satisfaction with the victim's death, and detailed knowledge of competition procedures that would facilitate the murder method."

"Not yet," Jackie agreed. "We need more than just a hostile lunch conversation and some bitter comments. But Wade Brooks just moved to the top of our suspect list."

"Above Smoke Jackson and Cassie Brennan?"

"Way above. Smoke had one grudge from three years ago. Wade has a pattern of grievances, current financial pressure, and what sounds like an escalating conflict with Tex over judging bias. Plus, his comment about Tex 'getting what was coming to him' was basically a confession of motive," Jackie explained.

"Statistical probability analysis supports this assessment," Melody added. "Wade Brooks meets all criteria for viable suspect with highest confidence levels in motive, means, and opportunity categories."

"So, what's our next step?"

Jackie was quiet for a moment, considering their options. "We need to find out more about Wade's financial situation, his recent interactions with Tex Morrison, and whether anyone saw him near the judging tent during critical time periods at the competition."

"How do we do that without tipping him off that we suspect him?"

"Very carefully," Jackie replied. "Because Wade Brooks is dangerous, and if he killed Tex Morrison, he won't hesitate to silence anyone who gets too close to the truth."

As Prairie Rose came into view, Jackie felt both relief at returning to familiar territory and determination to solve Tex Morrison's murder before anyone else got hurt. Wade Brooks might think he'd gotten away with the perfect revenge, but Jackie had spent years building cases against people who underestimated their opponents.

She wasn't about to let Uncle Charlie Joe's legacy be stained by association with a murderer's twisted sense of justice.

The investigation was far from over, but they finally had a suspect who fit all the criteria for someone capable of premeditated murder. Now they just had to prove it before Wade Brooks realized how much they knew about his motives and methods.

The afternoon sun cast long shadows across the Hill Country as they pulled into Charlie Joe's parking lot, and Jackie couldn't shake the feeling that those shadows might be hiding more danger than they realized.

Chapter Seven

The next morning arrived gray and drizzly, matching Jackie's mood as she made coffee in the small kitchenette of their apartment above the restaurant. She'd slept poorly, her mind churning through suspect profiles and unanswered questions about Tex Morrison's death. Lauren and Melody were already up, huddled over Melody's laptop at their tiny dining table.

"Any luck with the timeline mapping?" Jackie asked, settling beside them with her coffee.

"I've identified several critical gaps," Melody said, pointing to a detailed chart on her screen. "The period between 3:30 and 4:30 PM is particularly significant. That's when rib entries were being collected, transported to the judging tent and the judging was taking place."

"That's also when Cassie Brennan disappeared for about forty-five minutes," Lauren added. "I remember because she'd been constantly photographing everything all day, but suddenly she wasn't around during the first submission period."

Jackie studied the timeline. "Where did she go?"

"Unknown. She reappeared just as the pork submissions were happening at 5 PM, claiming she'd been uploading photos to her blog and doing interviews with spectators."

"We need to verify that," Jackie said. "Did anyone else notice her absence? Are there photos from that time period that show where she actually was?"

"I'm checking social media posts from other attendees," Melody said. "So far, no photos of Cassie between 3:30 and 4:30."

The sound of vehicles in the parking lot below drew their attention to the window. Despite the early hour and dismal weather, several cars were already arriving for what should have been the championship awards ceremony.

"Think people will still show up even though the competition was suspended?" Lauren asked.

"Some will want closure," Jackie said. "Others will be curious about the investigation. And a few might have information they want to share away from official police interviews."

A knock at their apartment door interrupted their conversation. Lauren opened it to find Sheriff Martinez standing on the landing with a white bakery box and an expression that mixed professional concern with personal warmth.

"Morning, ladies," he said, holding up the box. "Brought some of Mrs. Cohen's cinnamon rolls from the bakery. Thought you might need something sweet after yesterday's ordeal."

"That's very thoughtful," Lauren said, her face brightening at his presence. She stepped aside to let him in, and Jackie noticed how her sister unconsciously smoothed her hair and checked her appearance in the small mirror by the door.

"Coffee?" Jackie offered, already reaching for another mug.

"Please," Ray said, settling at their small dining table. He opened the bakery box to reveal eight perfect cinnamon rolls, their icing still slightly warm. "Mrs. Cohen insisted I bring extra. Said she heard about what happened and wanted to make sure all y'all were taken care of."

"The whole town's talking about it, isn't it?" Lauren asked, sitting across from Ray and accepting one of the pastries.

"People are concerned," Ray acknowledged. "Tex Morrison was respected, even by folks who didn't know him personally. Word of his murder has everyone on edge."

Jackie felt her stomach tighten at his choice of words. "Murder? You have confirmation it wasn't natural causes?"

They'd obviously assumed that was the case, but hearing his words made it real.

Ray's expression grew more serious, though he kept his voice gentle for Lauren's benefit. "The toxicology results came back early this morning. Tex was killed by a concentrated dose of oleander extract mixed into barbecue sauce."

"Oleander?" Lauren set down her coffee cup with trembling hands. "That's not accidental contamination."

"Definitely not. Oleander is extremely toxic, but it doesn't occur naturally in food preparation. Someone deliberately harvested and concentrated the poison, then found a way to get Tex to consume it."

Jackie's mind raced through implications while she watched Ray's attention focus on Lauren's obvious distress. His professional demeanor softened as he noticed her pale complexion and shaky hands.

"Lauren," he said quietly, "I know this is frightening. The idea that someone at the competition deliberately committed murder is hard to process."

"It's not just that," Lauren replied, meeting his concerned gaze. "It's the calculation involved. It wasn't just a crime of passion, a heat of the moment fight. Someone planned this for weeks, maybe months. They came to our competition with the specific intention of killing Tex."

"Which means they had detailed knowledge of competition procedures," Melody added, looking up from her laptop. "They'd have to know how judging worked, when entries were submitted, how to ensure Tex would consume the contaminated sauce."

Ray nodded, impressed by Melody's analytical approach. "That's exactly what we're thinking. The killer had to have insider knowledge of barbecue competitions, probably gained through direct participation or extensive research."

"Barbecue sauce narrows down the suspect pool significantly," Jackie observed. "Not every team uses sauce in their competition entries."

"Right. We're focusing on teams that submitted sauce-based entries and anyone who had access to the judging area where additional sauces were available for tasting." Ray pulled out a small notebook. "Which brings me to why I wanted to talk to you personally."

He looked directly at Lauren as he continued. "Your family isn't just potential witnesses anymore. Given your investigative background, someone might see you as a threat to their plans."

"What kind of threat?" Lauren asked, her voice tight with concern.

"The kind that gets eliminated to prevent exposure," Ray said bluntly, then immediately softened his tone as he saw Lauren's reaction. "I'm not trying to scare you unnecessarily, but I need you to understand that this situation could be more dangerous than it appears."

Jackie felt protective instincts flare as she watched her sister process this information. "What are you suggesting we do?"

"Be careful about who you trust with information. Don't investigate alone or put yourselves in isolated situations with potential suspects. And..." Ray hesitated, glancing between Jackie and Lauren, "keep me informed about anything unusual you notice or any approaches from strangers."

"Approaches?" Lauren asked.

"People asking questions about your family, your routines, your business operations. Anyone showing unusual interest in your activities or claiming to be reporters, researchers, insurance investigators. You know that kind of thing."

Ray reached across the table and gently covered Lauren's hand with his own, a gesture that was clearly personal rather than professional. "Lauren, I know we haven't known each other very long, but I want you to know that you can trust me completely. Both as sheriff and as..." he paused, searching for the right words, "as someone who cares about your well-being."

Lauren turned her hand palm up, briefly squeezing his fingers before he withdrew his hand. The brief contact carried more intimacy than any lengthy conversation could have conveyed.

"Ray," she said quietly, "does this investigation create problems for... whatever this is between us?"

"It creates complications," he acknowledged honestly. "I have to maintain professional objectivity, and I can't give your family any special treatment in the investigation. But it doesn't change my personal feelings."

Jackie cleared her throat gently, reminding them they weren't alone, and Ray straightened in his chair, his professional demeanor returning.

"The oleander extraction requires specific knowledge and equipment," he continued, consulting his notes. "You can't just boil the leaves and hope for the best. That would create an inconsistent concentration that might not be fatal. Whoever did this had chemistry knowledge or access to someone who did."

"So, we're looking for someone with scientific training?" Melody asked.

"Or someone who did extensive research on poison preparation. The internet makes that kind of information accessible, unfortunately."

"The barbecue sauce delivery method is clever," Jackie admitted with grudging professional respect. "Tex would naturally taste sauces during judging, and the strong flavors would help mask the bitter taste of oleander extract."

"Exactly. Which suggests the killer understood both Tex's judging habits and the sensory properties of oleander poisoning." Ray closed his notebook. "We're looking at someone who planned this murder very carefully, over an extended period of time."

As Ray prepared to leave, he lingered at the door, clearly reluctant to end his time with Lauren.

"The cinnamon rolls were a lovely thought," Lauren said, walking him to the apartment entrance. "Please thank Mrs. Cohen for us."

"I will. She's been asking about you since the competition. The whole town has, actually." Ray paused on the landing. "Lauren, would it be appropriate for me to check in with you regularly? Officially, I mean, to make sure you're safe and to get updates if you notice anything unusual."

"I think that would be very appropriate," Lauren replied, her smile suggesting she understood the personal motivations behind his official reasoning.

"Good. I'll stop by tomorrow evening, after my shift. Maybe we could talk on the porch, away from the pressure of investigation."

After Ray left, Jackie and Melody exchanged knowing glances as Lauren returned to the table with a distinctly pleased expression.

"He likes you," Melody observed matter-of-factly.

"The feeling appears to be mutual," Jackie added with amusement.

"He brought cinnamon rolls," Lauren said, as if that explained everything.

"He brought cinnamon rolls and important case information, stayed for an hour when he could have shared the toxicology results in a five-minute phone call, and arranged a reason to see you again tomorrow night," Jackie corrected. "That man is definitely interested."

"I like him," Lauren admitted, her cheeks slightly pink. "He's professional but not cold, protective without being controlling. And he brought pastries."

"Never underestimate a man who understands the importance of baked goods," Melody said solemnly, making both sisters laugh despite the serious circumstances they were discussing.

A knock at their apartment door interrupted the conversation. Jackie opened it to find Martin Delgado, the competition organizer, looking haggard and desperate.

"Ms. Prescott? I hope you don't mind me bothering you, but I need to talk to someone about yesterday. The police questions, the investigation. I'm worried they're going to blame me for what happened."

Jackie invited him in, noting how his hands shook as he accepted coffee from Lauren. Martin looked like he hadn't slept at all, and his usual confident demeanor had been replaced by obvious anxiety.

"Why would they blame you?" Jackie asked gently, though she should be asking why he felt the need to talk to them, but her curiosity at what information he might have won out.

"Because I was responsible for security, for managing the competition procedures, for making sure everything ran smoothly. If someone was able to poison a judge during my event..." He trailed off, staring into his coffee.

"Martin, you can't blame yourself for someone else's criminal actions," Lauren said. "You had no way to predict or prevent what happened."

"But maybe I did," Martin said quietly. "Maybe there were warning signs I should have noticed."

Jackie's attention sharpened. "What kind of warning signs?"

Martin was quiet for a long moment, clearly debating how much to reveal. "There had been... irregularities with some of the registration paperwork. Teams registering at the last minute, payment issues, questions about judging procedures that seemed unusually detailed."

"We registered last minute," Jackie observed.

"You did but it was different."

"Different how? What kinds of questions?" Melody asked.

"Specific questions about how entries are transported from cooking stations to judges, who handles the food during transit, whether judges taste entries in any particular order." Martin's voice grew more strained. "I thought they were just nervous first-time competitors wanting to understand the process."

"Which teams asked these questions?" Jackie pressed.

"That's just it. The questions came from multiple sources. Phone calls, emails, conversations during setup. I didn't think to connect them until after... until Tex died."

Jackie exchanged glances with Lauren. Someone had been conducting reconnaissance, gathering intelligence about competition procedures for weeks before the event.

"Do you have records of these communications?" she asked.

Martin nodded, pulling out his phone. "Email records, at least. Some of the phone calls were from blocked numbers."

As Martin scrolled through his emails, Jackie found herself thinking about the level of premeditation this suggested. The killer hadn't just decided to murder Tex Morrison at the competition, but they'd been planning it for weeks, maybe months.

"Here," Martin said, showing them an email from three weeks earlier. "This person wanted to know exactly how judging worked, whether entries were kept separate during transport, how judges coordinated their tasting schedule."

The email was from an address Jackie didn't recognize, but the questions were sophisticated. The kind of detailed inquiries someone would make if they were planning to manipulate the judging process.

"Did you respond to this?" she asked.

"I sent back our standard information packet about competition procedures. The same information we give to all competitors."

"But this person wasn't registered as a competitor?"

"Not at that time. They registered two days later under a different email address."

Melody looked up from her laptop where she'd been taking notes. "What name did they register under?"

Martin consulted his registration records. "C. Brennan. Paid the entry fee, submitted all required documentation, everything appeared legitimate."

"Cassie Brennan," Lauren said immediately.

"So, Cassie was researching competition procedures weeks in advance," Jackie concluded. "That's either very thorough preparation for legitimate competition, or detailed reconnaissance for murder planning."

"There's more," Martin said hesitantly. "I probably should have mentioned this to Sheriff Martinez, but I was hoping it wasn't important."

"What?" all three women asked simultaneously.

"Yesterday morning, before the competition started, I saw someone near Tex's RV who shouldn't have been there. It was early, maybe 6 AM, and most teams were still setting up. But this person was walking around the back of the judges' area like they were looking for something."

"Who was it?" Jackie asked, though she suspected she already knew.

"I couldn't see clearly in the dim light, but it looked like that food blogger. The blonde woman who was taking pictures all day."

Jackie felt puzzle pieces clicking into place. Cassie Brennan had been researching competition procedures for weeks, had disappeared during the critical submission period, and had been seen near Tex's RV early in the morning before the competition began.

"Martin," she said carefully, "I think you need to share this information with Sheriff Martinez. Today."

"Will they think I'm trying to deflect blame from myself?"

"They'll think you're providing important evidence that could help solve a murder," Lauren said firmly. "Tex Morrison deserves justice, and you're in a position to help provide it."

After Martin left to call Sheriff Martinez, the three women sat in contemplative silence.

"So, Cassie Brennan is looking more and more like our primary suspect," Lauren said finally.

"She had motive which was Tex's negative review damaged her business and credibility," Jackie agreed. "She had opportunity with access to the competition area and unaccounted for time during the critical period. And now we know she was conducting surveillance and reconnaissance."

"But we still don't know how she administered the poison. Did her team actually submit food? Did they have sauce on their food?" Melody asked. "How did she ensure Tex would consume the contaminated sauce?"

"That's what we need to figure out," Jackie said. "And we need to be very careful how we do it. If Cassie Brennan is a murderer, approaching her directly could be dangerous."

"So, what do we do?"

Jackie stood and walked to the window, looking down at the parking lot where more people were gathering despite the suspended competition. Among them, she could see several faces from yesterday, competitors who'd stayed in town, spectators who'd come for the awards ceremony, and media representatives following the story.

"We do what we do best," she said. "Lauren talks to people and gets them to trust her. Melody analyzes information and finds patterns. And I think like a prosecutor building a case."

"And Ray?" Lauren asked, a note of concern in her voice for the man who was clearly becoming important to her.

"Ray investigates this officially while we share information with him unofficially," Jackie replied.

As they prepared to go downstairs and begin their day of investigation, Jackie felt the familiar weight of responsibility. They'd committed themselves to finding Tex Morrison's killer, and she suspected they were closer to the truth than they realized.

The question now was whether they could prove Cassie Brennan's guilt without putting themselves in danger. Because if their theory was correct, they were dealing with someone who'd already killed once and might be willing to kill again to avoid being caught.

Chapter Eight

The restaurant's main dining room had been transformed into an unofficial gathering place for competitors and spectators who weren't ready to leave Prairie Rose. By mid-morning, nearly two dozen people had drifted in, seeking comfort food and the kind of community solidarity that emerges after shared trauma.

Their coffee pot was working overtime, and they were going through gallons of sweet tea. Mrs. Cohen sent over more of her warm cinnamon rolls for them to serve to anyone who wanted one until lunch service officially started.

Jackie worked the front counter while Lauren managed the kitchen with Jovie's help, but both sisters were listening carefully to conversations and watching for anything that might provide insight into Tex Morrison's murder.

"Terrible thing," said Frank Kowalski, their regular Tuesday customer who'd driven over specifically to check on them. "Tex Morrison was a good man. Whoever did this should be ashamed of themselves."

"Did you know him well?" Jackie asked as she poured Frank's sweet tea.

"Not personally, but by reputation. Fair judge, never took bribes, always gave honest critiques even when they hurt feelings. Made a lot of enemies that way but earned everyone's respect."

Jackie filed that information away. If Tex had a reputation for brutal honesty in his reviews, there could be multiple people with motives for revenge beyond just Cassie Brennan.

At a corner table, Billy "Smoke" Jackson sat with two other competitors, their voices carrying despite their attempts at discretion.

"I'm telling you, someone's trying to frame me," Smoke was saying. "All that talk yesterday about my grudge against Tex, making me look like the obvious suspect. But why would I kill him at a public competition where everyone would point fingers at me first?"

"Unless that's exactly what you wanted people to think," replied a woman Jackie didn't recognize. "Make it so obvious that investigators would assume you were too smart to do it that way."

"That's crazy talk," Smoke protested, but his voice carried an edge of desperation.

Jackie caught Lauren's eye and nodded toward Smoke's table. Her sister moved closer, wiping down nearby tables while listening to the conversation.

Shortly after, the front door opened and in walked Emma Barber with more confidence than she'd shown at the competition, carrying what appeared to be a covered dish. She looked around the crowded dining room.

"Emma," Lauren called out warmly. "What brings you by today?"

"Mom said you were experimenting with new side dish recipes," Emma replied, holding up the covered dish. "I thought I'd contribute to the research. It's my grandmother's recipe for German potato salad. Mom used to make it before I got sick, but I finally felt strong enough to tackle it myself. Plus, it looks as though you could use a little extra food."

Jovie emerged from the kitchen, her face lighting up at the sight of her daughter. "You didn't need to cook, honey. You're still building your strength back up."

"Mom, I'm feeling good. Really good. And I wanted to contribute something to the family business instead of just being the sick daughter." Emma's voice carried gentle determination. "Besides, cooking felt normal. It felt like moving forward instead of just recovering."

Jackie tasted the potato salad and found it perfectly balanced, tangy but not sharp, with herbs that complemented rather than competed with their barbecue flavors. "This is excellent. Would you be interested in helping us test other recipes? We've been talking about expanding our side dish options."

"I'd love that," Emma said, her enthusiasm evident. "I have about three to four hours of good energy most days now, and I'd rather spend it doing something useful than just sitting around celebrating being healthy."

"Three hours is perfect for recipe development," Melody observed practically. "That's enough time to test techniques without risking overexertion."

As they discussed potential collaboration, Jackie noticed how Emma's presence seemed to complete something in Jovie's demeanor. The careful reserve that had been part of Jovie's personality since they'd known her was softening into something warmer and more open.

"So, I'm officially part of the team now?" Emma asked with a smile that reminded Jackie strongly of her mother's rare moments of unguarded happiness.

"You've been part of the family," Lauren said firmly. "Now you get to be part of the daily work too."

They all got back to work with Emma joining Jovie in the kitchen. She seamlessly started portioning out sides including her German potato salad.

The front door chimed, and Melody looked up from the laptop where she'd been correlating competition data. "Mom, there's someone I want you to meet."

A young man about Melody's age entered, moving with the careful precision that Jackie had learned to recognize in people on the autism spectrum. He was tall and lean, with dark hair and the kind of focused intensity that reminded her of Melody when she was working through complex problems.

"This is Aiden Moss," Melody said, her voice carrying a note of excitement that Jackie rarely heard when her niece met new people. "His father competed yesterday with the River City Grilling team from San Antonio."

"Nice to meet you, Aiden," Lauren said warmly, approaching from the kitchen. "I'm Lauren, Melody's mom."

Aiden shook hands with careful formality. "Pleasure to meet you, Mrs. Beniot. Melody's been telling me about your investigation into Judge Morrison's murder. Her analytical approach is quite impressive."

Jackie raised an eyebrow at this. "Melody's been sharing our investigation?"

"Only the logical methodology," Melody said quickly. "Aiden has a master's degree in forensic science. He might be able to help us understand the technical aspects of the poisoning."

Aiden settled at the table with Melody, pulling out a notebook that was organized with the same systematic precision Jackie had come to associate with her niece. "I've been researching oleander toxicity since I heard about the murder method," he said. "There are some interesting aspects that might help narrow down the suspect pool."

"Such as?" Jackie asked, joining them at the table.

"Oleander extraction requires specific knowledge and equipment. You can't just boil the leaves and hope for the best. Doing that would create an inconsistent concentration that might not be fatal. Effective extraction requires understanding of alkaloid chemistry and access to proper processing equipment."

"So, we're looking for someone with scientific training?" Lauren asked.

"Or access to someone with scientific training," Aiden corrected. "The process isn't impossibly complex, but it's not something you'd figure out from a simple internet search."

Melody was taking notes as Aiden spoke, and Jackie noticed how naturally the two young people worked together, their conversation flowing with the kind of intellectual compatibility that was rare and precious. She looked over at Lauren who was watching the pair with a smile.

"There's another consideration," Aiden continued. "Oleander extract is extremely bitter, even more so than the natural plant. Masking that taste in barbecue sauce would require careful selection of flavoring agents and considerable testing to get the proportions right."

"Testing?" Jackie asked.

"The killer would need to experiment with different concentrations and flavor combinations to create something that would be palatable enough for a judge to consume without immediately detecting something wrong," Aiden explained. "That suggests advance preparation and probably multiple attempts to perfect the mixture."

"Which means potential evidence," Jackie realized. "Practice batches, discarded mixtures, maybe purchases of unusual ingredients."

"Exactly. This wasn't a spur-of-the-moment crime. Someone spent weeks or months preparing for this murder."

The conversation was interrupted by raised voices from Smoke Jackson's table. The argument had escalated, and other customers were beginning to stare.

"I don't care what you think," Smoke was saying loudly. "I had nothing to do with Tex's death, and I'm tired of everyone assuming I'm guilty just because we had a disagreement three years ago."

"Keep your voice down," hissed one of his companions. "You're not helping your case by making a scene."

"My case?" Smoke stood up abruptly, his chair scraping loudly against the floor. "This isn't a courtroom. I'm an innocent man whose reputation is being destroyed by gossip and assumptions."

He stormed toward the exit but paused at Jackie's table. "You ladies seem like fair people. I hope you're not buying into all the rumors about me wanting revenge on Tex Morrison."

"We're not buying into any rumors," Jackie said diplomatically. "We're just trying to understand what happened."

"What happened is that someone murdered a good man and tried to make it look like food poisoning so they could get away with it," Smoke said. "But it wasn't me, and I'll prove it if I have to."

After he left, the restaurant fell into uncomfortable silence.

"He seemed genuinely upset," Lauren observed quietly.

"Genuine emotion doesn't rule out guilt," Jackie replied. "Killers can feel bad about what they've done while still being killers."

"His point about the obviousness of his motive is interesting though," Melody said. "It would be unusually stupid to commit murder when you're the most likely suspect."

"Unless he's counting on that logic to protect him," Aiden suggested. "Reverse psychology, wanting to appear so obviously guilty that people assume you must be innocent."

Before anyone could respond, Cassie Brennan entered the restaurant, her professional smile firmly in place despite the previous day's tragedy. She carried her camera and moved through the dining room taking photos as if nothing had changed.

"Good morning, everyone," she announced brightly. "I hope you don't mind if I capture some images of the community coming together after yesterday's unfortunate event. My readers are very interested in how small towns handle crisis situations."

Jackie felt her jaw tighten at Cassie's casual reference to murder as an "unfortunate event," but she kept her expression neutral.

Cassie approached their table, camera raised. "The family restaurant owners providing comfort to grieving competitors. This is exactly the kind of heartwarming story my audience loves."

"We'd prefer not to be photographed today," Lauren said firmly.

"Of course, of course. I understand completely." Cassie lowered her camera but didn't move away. "Such a tragedy about Judge Morrison. I've been researching his background for a memorial piece, and it's fascinating how many people had... complicated relationships with him."

"What do you mean?" Melody asked.

"Well, Tex was known for his honest critiques, but honest can sometimes cross the line into cruel. I've found at least six restaurants that closed within a year of receiving negative reviews from him." Cassie's voice carried false sympathy. "It makes you wonder how many people might have harbored resentment."

"Are you suggesting Tex deserved to die because he gave honest reviews?" Jackie asked, not bothering to hide her distaste.

"No, of course not," Cassie said quickly. "I'm just observing that his murder might have more potential suspects than people realize. It would be a shame if someone like Smoke Jackson was convicted simply because he's the obvious choice, while the real killer went free."

"Do you have information about other suspects?" Lauren asked.

Cassie smiled mysteriously. "Let's just say my research has uncovered some interesting connections between Judge Morrison and various people in the barbecue community. Connections that go deeper than professional disagreements."

She moved away before they could ask follow-up questions, continuing her photography tour of the dining room while making notes in a small notebook.

"I don't like her," Aiden said quietly. "Her questions yesterday during the competition were oddly specific, and her behavior today seems calculated to deflect suspicion from herself."

"You noticed her yesterday?" Jackie asked.

"She interviewed my father's team around noon. Asked detailed questions about our cooking methods, our equipment, whether we'd had any interactions with the judges." Aiden consulted his notebook. "She also wanted to know if we'd observed anything unusual about the judging procedures."

"Did you?"

"Actually, yes. Around 4:15, I saw someone in the judging tent who shouldn't have been there. One of the volunteers was arguing with someone about proper procedure, but I couldn't see who it was from my angle."

Melody leaned forward with interest. "What time exactly?"

"4:17 PM. I noted it because we had just submitted our ribs, and we were preparing our pork. I was tracking all the timing carefully."

Jackie felt a surge of excitement. 4:17 PM was right in the middle of the window when Cassie Brennan had been missing from her usual photography routine.

"Could you identify the person who was arguing with the volunteer?" she asked.

"Not definitively, but they appeared to be female, medium height, blonde hair. The volunteer kept saying 'you can't be in here' and 'this area is restricted to authorized personnel only.'"

"That sounds like it could have been Cassie," Lauren said.

"It's circumstantial, but it places someone matching her description in the judging area during the critical time period," Jackie agreed. "We need to find that volunteer and see if they can provide a positive identification."

As the day progressed and more competitors shared their stories, a complex picture began to emerge. Tex Morrison had indeed made enemies through his brutally honest reviews, but he'd also helped launch the careers of numerous pitmasters by recognizing genuine talent and technique.

"The man was complicated," admitted Pete Kowalski, one of the older competitors. "Tough as nails in his judging, but generous with advice if you asked him for help. I've seen him spend two hours teaching a young pitmaster how to manage temperature control, then give that same person a failing score the next day when their brisket was overcooked."

"Sounds like he separated personal relationships from professional standards," Jackie observed.

"Exactly. Which is why this murder doesn't make sense as simple revenge for a bad review. Tex's critiques were harsh but fair, and most serious competitors understood that."

As the lunch crowd began to thin out, Jackie found herself more convinced than ever that Tex Morrison's murder was about something more complex than professional grievances or wounded pride.

The killer had invested considerable time and effort in planning the murder, had extensive knowledge of competition procedures, and had been able to access the judging area during the critical time period. That suggested someone with both strong motive and significant resources.

Cassie Brennan still looked like their best suspect with Wade Brooks being a close second, but Jackie's legal instincts warned her against focusing too narrowly on any single theory. Real murderers were often more clever than they initially appeared, and the obvious suspect wasn't always the guilty one.

They needed more evidence before they could be confident in their conclusions. And they needed to be very careful about how they gathered that evidence, because if their suspicions were correct, they were investigating someone who'd already killed once and might not hesitate to kill again.

Chapter Nine

After the lunch crowd dispersed, Melody found herself alone with Aiden in the restaurant's dining room, both of them surrounded by notebooks, printouts, and laptops displaying various research findings. Jackie and Lauren had gone to interview some of the competing teams at their motels, leaving Melody to continue her timeline analysis.

"Your organizational system is fascinating," Aiden observed, studying the color-coded charts Melody had spread across three tables. "I've never seen anyone map temporal data quite this way."

Melody felt warmth spread through her chest, a sensation she'd learned to recognize as pleasure at being understood. Most people found her systematic approaches excessive or strange, but Aiden was examining her work with genuine appreciation.

"I assign different colors to different types of activities," she explained, pointing to her legend. "Blue for competitor movements, green for volunteer activities, red for anything involving the judges, yellow for external people like media or spectators."

"And the thickness of the lines indicates duration of activity?"

"Exactly. So, you can see at a glance that Cassie Brennan's absence, this thick red line, coincides precisely with the rib submission period and the gap in volunteer supervision near the judging tent."

Aiden leaned closer to study her chart, and Melody caught the clean scent of his soap mixed with something that might have been coffee. The proximity didn't make her uncomfortable the way it usually did with strangers, which was unusual enough to be noteworthy.

"Have you considered mapping the physical space as well as the temporal sequence?" he asked. "An overhead view of the competition area with movement patterns overlay might reveal additional insights."

"I started one," Melody said, pulling out her laptop. "But I don't have accurate measurements of distances between stations."

"I do." Aiden opened his own notebook to reveal detailed sketches of the competition layout, complete with measurements and notations. "I always map unfamiliar environments for better spatial processing. Want to combine our data?"

For the next hour, they worked together to create a comprehensive visualization that showed both when events occurred and where they took place. Melody found herself relaxing into the collaborative rhythm in ways she rarely experienced with other people.

"You measured the distance between every cooking station and the judging tent?" she asked, impressed by the thoroughness of his spatial documentation.

"Spatial relationships affect timing and opportunity," Aiden replied matter-of-factly. "If we know Cassie Brennan was at position X at time Y, we can calculate whether she could have reached position Z by time W."

"That's brilliant. I focus too much on temporal sequences and not enough on spatial logistics."

"And I sometimes get lost in physical details and miss temporal patterns. We complement each other well."

The comment hung between them with a significance that felt both comfortable and thrilling. Melody glanced at Aiden and found him watching her with an expression of gentle interest that made her stomach flutter in entirely pleasant ways.

"Found something," she said, turning back to their combined visualization to cover her sudden shyness. "Look at this movement pattern."

Their analysis showed that between 4:10 and 4:25 PM, when rib entries were being collected and transported to judges, there had been a fifteen-minute window when the normal volunteer supervision was disrupted.

"The volunteer who was supposed to monitor entry transport went to help with a propane leak at one of the cooking stations," Melody explained, tracing the movement pattern on their map. "That left the judging area temporarily unsupervised."

"And both Cassie Brennan and Wade Brooks were unaccounted for during that exact same period," Aiden added. "Either of them could have accessed the judging tent, contaminated one of the sauce containers, and been gone before normal supervision resumed."

"But how would they know about the propane leak in advance? That seems like it would be random timing."

Aiden was quiet for a moment, studying their timeline. "Unless it wasn't random. What if they created the propane leak specifically to draw the volunteer away from his post?"

Melody felt excitement building as the implications became clear. "A deliberate distraction to create opportunity. That would require advanced knowledge of the competition setup and volunteer assignments."

"Which brings us back to those detailed questions she was asking Martin Delgado about competition procedures."

"And Wade has advanced knowledge of competition procedures already," Melody added.

They spent another thirty minutes refining their analysis, and Melody found herself enjoying not just the intellectual challenge but also Aiden's company in ways she'd never experienced with someone she'd just met. He understood her need for systematic approaches, didn't find her detailed questions annoying, and contributed insights that genuinely improved their work.

"Melody," he said suddenly, "can I ask you something personal?"

She tensed slightly, as personal questions usually led to awkward territory about her autism or her family's unusual situation.

"Are you planning to stay in Prairie Rose permanently, or is this temporary while you help your family with the restaurant?"

The question surprised her with its thoughtfulness. Most people asked invasive questions about her "condition" or her ability to live independently. Aiden was asking about her future plans as if they mattered to him personally.

"I haven't decided," she admitted. "I love the work at the restaurant, and I love living close to Mom and Aunt Jackie. But I sometimes wonder if I should pursue more formal education or career development. Mom worries about me, but I want her to see I can be more independent."

"What would you want to study?"

"Forensic science, actually. Or maybe criminal justice with a focus on analytical methodologies. This investigation has made me realize how much I enjoy applying systematic analysis to complex problems."

Aiden's face lit up with genuine enthusiasm. "You'd be excellent at forensic science. Your attention to detail, your pattern recognition abilities, your systematic thinking, those are exactly the skills that make great forensic analysts."

"Really?"

"Really. I've met a lot of forensic science students and professionals, and most of them would kill for your natural analytical abilities."

The word "kill" hung in the air for a moment, reminding them both of the reason they were working together.

"Speaking of killing," Melody said, attempting to redirect the conversation back to safer territory, "should we try to verify our theory about the propane leak distraction?"

"Definitely. We need to identify which team had the leak and find out exactly what caused it."

Melody consulted her notes from the previous day's conversations. "Three teams mentioned equipment problems during the competition. Two had temperature control issues, and one, let me find it, yes, the Austin Smoke Masters had a propane regulator problem around 4 PM."

"Austin Smoke Masters," Aiden repeated. "That's interesting. Cassie Brennan is from Austin. She might have connections to that team and if they were located near her own team."

"We should find out if she knew them personally before the competition."

As they prepared to contact the Austin team, Melody realized she felt more energized and focused than she had in weeks. Working with someone who understood her thinking patterns, who appreciated her analytical approaches, and who contributed genuine insights was proving to be both professionally valuable and personally fulfilling.

"Aiden," she said impulsively, "would you like to have dinner with me tonight? Somewhere other than the restaurant, I mean. Just to talk about... things other than murder investigations."

His smile was warm and slightly shy. "I'd like that very much. Do you know any quiet places in town? I'm not great with crowds or loud environments."

"I know exactly the place," Melody said, feeling a flutter of anticipation mixed with nervous excitement. "There's a small café that serves excellent soup and stays quiet even during dinner hours."

"That sounds perfect."

As they continued working on their investigation, Melody found herself looking forward to evening with an anticipation she'd never experienced before. She'd always assumed that romantic relationships would be too complicated and unpredictable for someone with her needs and preferences. But Aiden seemed to understand her social patterns, appreciated her intellectual approaches, and made her feel comfortable in her own skin.

"Found the Austin Smoke Masters' contact information," she announced, refocusing on their current task. "Want to call them together?"

"Absolutely," Aiden said. "Though we should probably rehearse our approach. We don't want to sound like we're accusing them of anything."

"Just gathering information about the timeline of equipment problems during the competition," Melody agreed. "Completely legitimate research that has nothing to do with suspecting anyone of murder."

"Exactly. We're just two analytical people trying to understand the sequence of events."

As they prepared for the phone call, Melody reflected on how much her life had changed since inheriting Uncle Charlie Joe's restaurant. Six months ago, she'd been isolated and uncertain about her future. Now she was part of a family business, contributing to a murder investigation, and possibly beginning her first romantic relationship.

The future felt full of possibilities in ways that both excited and terrified her. But with Aiden beside her, approaching challenges with the same systematic methods she relied on, even the uncertainty felt manageable.

They were about to make the call to Austin Smoke Masters when Jackie and Lauren returned from their motel interviews, looking pleased with themselves.

"Learn anything interesting?" Melody asked.

"Very interesting," Jackie said. "And from the looks of your charts and maps, you two have been busy as well."

"We have a theory about how Cassie Brennan created the opportunity to access the judging tent," Aiden said. "But we need to verify some details about equipment problems during the competition."

"Equipment problems?" Lauren asked. "That's funny. Two of the teams we interviewed mentioned seeing Cassie Brennan near their cooking stations right before they had technical difficulties."

Melody and Aiden exchanged significant glances. Their theory about deliberate distraction was looking more plausible by the minute.

"I think," Jackie said slowly, "we need to have a very careful conversation about what we're discovering. Because if Cassie Brennan was systematically creating distractions and manipulating competition procedures, we're dealing with someone who's been planning this murder for a very long time."

Melody felt a chill of apprehension mixed with intellectual excitement. They were getting close to solving the case, but they were also realizing just how dangerous their suspect might be.

Chapter Ten

Melody woke the next morning with an unfamiliar sense of contentment that took her a moment to identify. The dinner with Aiden had been... perfect wasn't quite the right word, since Melody didn't believe in perfection, but it had been remarkably comfortable and engaging in ways she'd never experienced before.

They'd spent three hours at Susie's Café talking about everything except murder investigations. Everything from forensic science techniques, spatial analysis applications, their shared appreciation for systematic approaches to complex problems, and their mutual struggles with social environments that didn't accommodate their processing styles.

"How was your evening?" Lauren asked quietly as Melody joined her in the apartment's small kitchen.

"Educational," Melody replied, which was her standard response to new experiences. But then she found herself adding, "Also pleasant. Aiden understands how I think about things."

Lauren's smile was warm and knowing. "That's important. Finding someone who appreciates your mind instead of trying to change it."

"He asked if he could help with our investigation today. He has some ideas about verifying the propane leak timeline."

"I'd like that. Fresh perspectives are always valuable, especially from someone with forensic training."

They were preparing coffee when Jackie emerged from her room. "Any new developments while I was unconscious?"

"Aiden and I confirmed our theory about the Austin Smoke Masters' equipment failure," Melody said, consulting the notebook where she'd summarized their previous day's findings. "The propane regulator problem occurred at exactly 4:13 PM, which correlates perfectly with the gap in volunteer supervision at the judging tent."

"And?" Jackie asked, pouring herself coffee.

"And the team leader specifically remembered seeing Cassie Brennan near their equipment about ten minutes before the problem started. She was supposedly photographing their setup, but she spent an unusual amount of time examining their propane connections."

Jackie's expression sharpened with interest. "She could have loosened the regulator just enough to cause a slow leak that would become problematic during peak cooking time."

"That's our theory. Create a deliberate distraction that would pull the volunteer away from the judging area, then use the window of opportunity to contaminate one of the sauce containers."

A knock at their apartment door interrupted the conversation. Lauren opened it to find Tom Whitfield standing on the landing, hat in his hands and an expression of deep trouble on his weathered face.

"Morning, ladies. Hope I'm not intruding, but I need to talk to y'all about my cousin Tex. There are some things about his death that don't sit right with me."

Jackie invited Tom in, noting how his usual confident demeanor had been replaced by something that looked like guilt mixed with anger.

Blue immediately settled into his now-familiar position beside Melody's chair, close enough that his steady breathing provided a calming rhythm while she processed the complex information Tom was sharing. Melody found herself unconsciously resting one hand on Blue's head, the repetitive motion of stroking his fur helping her mind organize the mounting details of criminal conspiracy and systematic corruption.

"I've been thinking about what happened at the competition," Tom said, settling heavily into one of their small dining chairs. "And I realize I might know something important that I didn't think to mention to Sheriff Martinez, but I will. I just want to talk it out."

"What kind of something?" Lauren asked, pouring Tom a cup of coffee.

"Tex called me three days before the competition. Said he was worried about some irregularities he'd noticed in recent judging events. Asked if I'd ever heard rumors about judges being pressured or bribed to change their scores."

Melody looked up from her notebook. "What kind of irregularities?"

"Tex said some recent competitions had results that didn't match his expectations based on the quality of entries he'd tasted. Winners who shouldn't have won, established pitmasters scoring lower than their skills warranted." Tom's jaw tightened. "He thought someone might be manipulating the judging process for financial gain."

"Financial gain how?" Jackie asked.

"Betting pools, sponsorship deals, equipment endorsements. There's serious money in competition barbecue these days, and if someone could predict or control the results..." Tom shrugged. "Lot of ways to profit from that kind of information."

"Did Tex mention specific competitions or judges?" Lauren asked.

"He was being careful about accusations, but he'd been keeping notes. Said he had documentation of suspicious patterns going back at least six months."

Jackie felt puzzle pieces shifting into new configurations. "Where are those notes now?"

"That's what I'm wondering. Tex always carried a small notebook where he recorded his judging observations. I didn't see it among his belongings when the sheriff inventoried his RV."

As Tom described Tex's missing documentation, Melody's analytical processing began to accelerate, and Blue immediately sensed the shift in her stress levels. The dog adjusted his position to press more firmly against her leg, providing the kind of steady pressure that helped ground her when information became overwhelming.

Melody appreciated how Blue had learned to read her subtle cues and respond with exactly the right amount of calming contact.

"You think someone took it?" Melody asked.

"I think if Tex had evidence of judging corruption, that would be a powerful motive for murder. And if the killer knew about his documentation, they'd make sure to destroy it."

Tom pulled out his phone and showed them a text message. "This is what Tex sent me the night before he died: 'Found smoking gun. Will expose everything after Prairie Rose judging. Too dangerous to act sooner.'"

The room fell silent as the implications sank in.

Blue's ears pricked up at the change in the room's emotional atmosphere, and he lifted his head to assess each person's stress level before returning his attention to Melody, who was rapidly taking notes while processing the revelation about Tex's planned exposure.

The dog seemed to understand that his primary job was to keep Melody anchored during these intense investigative discussions.

"He was planning to reveal the corruption after the competition," Jackie said slowly. "Which means the killer had to act during the competition to prevent that exposure."

"And it means this wasn't just about Cassie Brennan's restaurant review," Lauren added. "This was about protecting a larger criminal conspiracy."

Tom nodded grimly. "Tex was always too honest for his own good. If he'd discovered systematic corruption in competition judging, he'd never have kept quiet about it, no matter who it implicated."

"But how does Cassie Brennan fit into a judging corruption scheme?" Melody asked. "She's a food blogger, not a judge."

"Media influence," Jackie suggested. "Food bloggers with large followings can affect public perception, sponsor interest, even competition attendance. If someone was manipulating results, they'd want media allies who could help control the narrative."

"Or maybe she discovered the corruption and was being paid to keep quiet about it," Lauren suggested. "Blackmail could be more profitable than legitimate blogging."

Tom finished his coffee, and Lauren automatically poured him more. He nodded thanks. "I should have told Sheriff Martinez about Tex's suspicions immediately. I was hoping his death really was just random food poisoning, but..."

"But you know it wasn't," Jackie completed.

"I know my cousin. Tex was careful about food safety, careful about everything. Someone wanted him dead before he could expose what he'd discovered." Tom's voice carried the weight of family loyalty and personal guilt. "I failed him by not taking his concerns more seriously when he was alive."

"You can still help him now by sharing what you know with Ray," Lauren said gently. "And with us, if you're willing."

"What else do you need to know?"

"Everything Tex told you about the corruption, everyone he suspected, any patterns he mentioned in the irregularities he'd noticed," Jackie said. "Also, anything you know about his relationships with other judges, competition organizers, or media people in the barbecue world."

Tom spent the next hour providing a detailed account of his conversations with Tex over the past several months. The picture that emerged was of a respected judge who'd become increasingly troubled by what he perceived as systematic manipulation of competition results.

Throughout Tom's detailed recounting, Melody systematically recorded every significant detail while Blue maintained his steady presence beside her. Occasionally, when her notetaking became particularly rapid, a sign of stress-driven hyperfocus, Blue would gently nudge her free hand, reminding her to take breaks and maintain awareness of her physical comfort. The subtle intervention had become such a natural part of their routine that Melody barely registered it consciously, but it consistently helped her maintain sustainable concentration during extended information processing sessions.

Lauren noticed and made note of it each time he did it. It was fascinating to watch the dog understand her so well. Usually, that was Lauren's job and if she missed any sign, it could lead to a complete meltdown. Blue, on the other hand, never missed a sign which was what caught Lauren's attention most.

"Tex mentioned that someone had approached him about six weeks ago," Tom said. "Wanted to discuss 'mutually beneficial arrangements' regarding his judging decisions. He told them he wasn't interested and reported the contact to the competition association."

"Did he say who approached him?" Melody asked.

"He didn't give me the name, just someone claiming to represent sponsor interests, but Tex thought it was more than that. Said the person knew too much about specific judging procedures and had access to information that should have been confidential."

"Like what kind of information?"

"Judge assignments for upcoming competitions, details about scoring protocols, even personal information about judges' financial situations." Tom's expression darkened. "Tex felt like he was being evaluated as a potential target for corruption."

"That's significant information to this," Jackie noted.

"I agree which is why I realized I need to call the sheriff." He stood. "Thanks for letting me talk this out. Come on, Blue."

The dog looked at Melody but then joined his owner.

After Tom left, the three women sat in contemplative silence, processing the new information.

"So, we have two potential motives for Tex's murder," Jackie summarized. "Cassie Brennan's personal revenge for the bad review, and a larger conspiracy to prevent him from exposing judging corruption."

"Or both," Lauren suggested. "Maybe Cassie was part of the corruption scheme and killed Tex to protect the conspiracy as well as herself."

"That would explain the level of premeditation," Melody observed. "Systematic reconnaissance, detailed planning, sophisticated poison preparation. This wasn't just personal revenge. It was professional elimination of a threat to a criminal organization."

They moved downstairs to start prepping for the day.

Shortly after they finished getting all the meat in the smoker, Aiden arrived, carrying a folder of research materials and wearing the focused expression Melody had learned to associate with significant discoveries.

"I've been researching competition results from the past year," he announced, settling at their table and opening his folder. "Looking for the kinds of statistical anomalies that might indicate manipulation."

"What did you find?" Jackie asked.

"Three competitions where the results don't match expected probability distributions based on historical performance data," Aiden said, spreading out charts and graphs. "Teams that consistently placed in middle rankings suddenly winning major competitions, established champions scoring unusually low, scoring patterns that suggest non-random judging decisions."

"And Tex Morrison was a judge at all three competitions?" Lauren asked.

"Yes, but not the only consistent factor." Aiden pointed to another chart. "Martin Delgado organized two of the three events. And Cassie Brennan provided media coverage for all three, including extensive social media promotion of the unexpected winners."

Melody felt the familiar thrill of pattern recognition. "We're seeing systematic coordination between competition organizer, media coverage, and judging results. That's not coincidence."

"It's a criminal conspiracy," Jackie agreed. "And Tex Morrison was about to expose all of it."

As they continued analyzing Aiden's research, Melody found herself impressed once again by his methodical approach and thorough documentation. Working with someone who shared her appreciation for systematic analysis was proving both professionally valuable and personally satisfying.

"There's one more thing," Aiden said quietly. "I found evidence that Cassie Brennan's restaurant received a significant cash infusion about two months after the first suspicious competition. Fifty thousand dollars listed as an 'investment from anonymous sponsor.'"

"Payment for services rendered," Jackie concluded grimly.

They now had motive, means, opportunity, and evidence of a broader criminal conspiracy. But they still needed proof that would hold up in court, and they still needed to be very careful about how they gathered that proof.

Because if their theory was correct, they weren't just investigating a single murder. They were uncovering a criminal organization that had already killed once to protect their secrets and wouldn't hesitate to kill again.

Chapter Eleven

The revelation about systematic competition corruption had transformed their investigation from a simple murder case into something much more complex and dangerous. Jackie found herself pacing the small apartment, her legal mind working through the implications of what they'd uncovered.

"If we're right about this being a criminal organization," she said, pausing by the window to look down at the restaurant parking lot, "then Tex's murder was just damage control. There are probably other victims we don't know about."

"Other judges who refused to cooperate?" Lauren suggested.

"Or competitors who asked too many questions, media people who wouldn't play along, anyone who threatened to expose the scheme." Jackie turned back to the room where Melody and Aiden were still analyzing competition data. "What's the scope of this thing? How many competitions, how much money, how many people involved?"

Aiden pulled up a spreadsheet on his laptop. "Based on the statistical anomalies I've identified, potentially dozens of competitions over the past two years. Between prize money, sponsorship deals, betting pools, we could be looking at millions of dollars in fraudulent activity."

"And that's just what we can detect from public records," Melody added. "The real financial impact could be much larger if there are private betting operations or undisclosed sponsorship arrangements."

Lauren's phone buzzed with a text from Sheriff Martinez: *Need to talk. I'll stop by shortly.*

Lauren simply replied with okay.

"Ray wants to see us," she told Jackie, showing her the message.

"About our investigation or about something else?" Jackie asked, concern creeping into her voice.

"Unknown. But the timing suggests he might have learned something significant about the case."

Before anyone could speculate further, Jackie's phone rang. The caller ID showed Harold Westin, their family lawyer who'd handled Uncle Charlie Joe's estate.

"Harold? What's going on?"

"Jackie, I need to ask you something, and I need you to be completely honest with me." Harold's voice carried an urgency she'd never heard from him before. "Have you been investigating Tex Morrison's murder?"

"Why do you ask?"

"Because someone called my office this morning asking detailed questions about your family's legal representation, your financial situation, and whether you might be vulnerable to lawsuits or criminal charges related to the competition."

Jackie felt cold dread settle in her stomach. "Who was asking these questions?"

"The caller claimed to be a journalist researching the murder case, but their questions were more like what you'd expect from someone building a legal attack strategy. They wanted to know about your divorce settlement, your professional liability insurance, whether you had any history of food safety violations at the restaurant."

"Did you give them any information?"

"Of course not. Attorney-client privilege applies even to general inquiries. But Jackie, this feels like someone trying to find ways to discredit you or create legal problems for your family."

"Because we're getting too close to something they want to keep hidden?"

"That would be my interpretation. Be very careful, and document everything you're doing. If someone's building a case against you, you'll need solid records of your investigative methods and findings."

After Harold hung up, Jackie shared the conversation with the others. The news added another layer of concern to their already dangerous situation.

"They're trying to neutralize us," Lauren said quietly. "Turn us from investigators into suspects or targets."

"Which means we're definitely onto something important," Melody observed with her characteristic matter-of-fact tone.

"Criminal organizations don't waste resources trying to discredit people who aren't threats to them."

"But it also means we need to be much more careful," Jackie said. "If they're willing to research our legal vulnerabilities, they might be planning more direct action."

Aiden had been quietly working on his laptop during this conversation, but now he looked up with an expression of excitement mixed with concern.

"I found something else," he announced. "A pattern in the timing of suspicious competition results that correlates with major betting events and sponsorship announcements."

He turned his screen so they could see a complex timeline showing competition dates, unusual results, and financial events.

"Look at this sequence: suspicious results at the East Texas Regional, followed within two weeks by major sponsorship deals for the unexpected winners, followed by those same sponsors placing large bets on those teams at subsequent competitions."

"It's a cycle," Melody realized, studying the pattern. "Manipulate results to create artificial reputation for certain teams, then profit from sponsorship and betting on those teams' continued success."

"Exactly. And the profits from each cycle fund the next round of corruption becoming bribes for judges, payments to media for favorable coverage, money for competition organizers to ensure cooperation."

"How much money are we talking about?" Jackie asked.

"Based on publicly available information about sponsorship deals and prize distributions, probably at least two million dollars over the past eighteen months. But if there are private betting operations or undisclosed financial arrangements, the real number could be much higher."

Lauren was studying the timeline with growing concern. "This level of organization and financial coordination, we're not just dealing with a few bad actors. This is a professional criminal operation."

"Which makes Tex Morrison's murder even more significant," Jackie said. "They didn't kill him in a moment of passion or panic. They eliminated a threat to a multi-million-dollar criminal enterprise."

"And now we're the threat," Melody said quietly.

Before anyone could respond, they heard vehicles pulling into the parking lot below. Jackie looked out the window to see two unmarked sedans and Sheriff Martinez's patrol car arriving simultaneously.

"That's either very good news or very bad news," she said.

A few minutes later, Sheriff Martinez knocked on their apartment door, accompanied by two people Jackie didn't recognize, a woman in her fifties wearing a business suit and a younger man with the alert posture of someone in law enforcement.

"Ladies, I'd like you to meet Agent Sarah Reeves from the FBI Financial Crimes Division and Detective Mike Sullivan from the Texas Rangers," Martinez said. "We need to talk about your investigation into Tex Morrison's murder."

Jackie felt a mixture of relief and apprehension. Federal involvement suggested they'd been right about the scope of the criminal organization, but it also meant they were in much deeper water than they'd realized.

"Agent Reeves," Jackie said, inviting them into the small apartment. "I assume this visit means you've discovered the same corruption patterns we've been investigating."

"Actually, we've been investigating this criminal organization for six months," Reeves replied, settling at their dining table. "Tex Morrison was one of our confidential informants."

The room fell silent as the implications hit them.

"Tex was working undercover?" Lauren asked.

"Not exactly undercover, but he was documenting evidence for us and reporting on attempts to corrupt his judging decisions," Detective Sullivan explained. "We've been building a case against what we believe is a multi-state operation involving competition manipulation, illegal gambling, and money laundering."

"And now your key witness is dead," Jackie said.

"Yes, which is why your investigation is so valuable," Agent Reeves said. "You've independently identified many of the same patterns and connections we've been tracking. Your research has actually provided us with several new leads."

Melody looked up from her notebook where she'd been taking notes. "Does this mean we're in danger for continuing our investigation?"

"Potentially, yes. The phone call to your lawyer suggests they're already trying to neutralize you through legal intimidation. If that doesn't work, they might escalate to more direct methods."

"So, what do we do?" Lauren asked.

"You continue your investigation, but you do it in coordination with us," Agent Reeves said. "We provide protection and resources, you provide local knowledge and the kind of access we can't get through official channels."

"What kind of access?" Jackie asked.

"The barbecue competition community is tight-knit and suspicious of outsiders, especially law enforcement," Detective Sullivan explained. "But they trust you because you're part of the community now. They'll share information with you that they'd never share with us."

Agent Reeves opened a briefcase and pulled out a thick folder. "We'd like to show you what we've learned about the criminal organization you've been investigating. It's larger and more sophisticated than you probably realize."

As they spread documents across the table, Jackie began to understand the true scope of what they were dealing with. The competition corruption was just one part of a complex operation that included illegal gambling, tax evasion, and money laundering through legitimate barbecue businesses.

"The ringleader is someone with deep connections throughout the barbecue world," Agent Reeves explained. "Someone who's been building this network for years, carefully recruiting judges, competitors, organizers, and media people."

"Do you know who it is?" Aiden asked.

"We have strong suspicions, but not enough evidence for prosecution yet. That's where your investigation becomes crucial. You've been able to gather information and make connections that our official investigation couldn't access."

"What about Wade Brooks?" Jackie asked. "We visited his restaurant yesterday, and he made some pretty hostile comments about Tex Morrison. Plus, he had clear access to the judging area during the competition."

Agent Reeves consulted her notes. "Wade Brooks... yes, we've noted him as a person of interest. Local restaurant owner with financial struggles and documented hostility toward the victim. He's definitely on our list for follow-up investigation."

"Financial struggles?" Lauren asked.

"Brooks' Barbecue Barn has been losing money for the past two years. Declining customer base, increased competition, some tax issues. Desperate business owners sometimes make desperate choices."

"What do you need from us?" Jackie asked.

"Keep doing what you're doing but share everything you discover with us immediately. Don't confront suspected participants directly, and don't take any risks that could compromise your safety."

"And in exchange?"

"We provide federal protection for your family and full resources for solving Tex Morrison's murder," Detective Sullivan said. "Plus, when we bring down this organization, you'll have the satisfaction of knowing you helped bring justice for your friend."

As the federal agents prepared to leave, Agent Reeves handed Jackie a secure phone. "Direct line to our task force. Use it if you discover anything significant or if you feel threatened in any way."

After they left, the four of them sat in contemplative silence, processing the magnitude of what they'd learned.

"We're now part of a federal investigation into a multi-million-dollar criminal organization," Lauren said finally.

"Which means we're both more protected and more at risk than we were this morning," Jackie added.

"But we're also much more likely to get justice for Tex Morrison," Melody pointed out. "And to prevent other people from being victimized by this corruption."

"Plus," Aiden said with a slight smile, "we get to keep investigating, but now we have federal backup if things get dangerous."

Jackie looked around their small apartment, thinking about how much their lives had changed. They'd started as amateur investigators trying to solve a single murder, and now they were key assets in a federal investigation of organized crime.

Uncle Charlie Joe would probably be proud of them for refusing to back down when things got complicated. But he'd also want them to be smart about protecting themselves and each other.

The criminal organization they were investigating had already killed once, that they knew of, to protect their secrets. With federal involvement, the stakes had just gotten much higher for everyone involved.

"Tomorrow," Jackie said, "we start working with the FBI to take down whoever killed Tex Morrison. But tonight, we make sure our security is solid, and our family is safe."

"Agreed," Lauren said.

"And we celebrate the fact that we're fighting for justice with federal resources backing us up," Melody added.

"And we remember that Uncle Charlie Joe taught us to take care of each other no matter what," Jackie concluded.

As they prepared for what was likely to be a very challenging and dangerous period ahead, Jackie felt both apprehensive and determined. They were about to take on a criminal organization that had been operating with impunity for years.

But they weren't doing it alone anymore.

Chapter Twelve

The next morning brought the familiar rhythm of restaurant preparation, and Jackie found herself grateful for the comforting routine of starting fires, checking temperatures, and organizing ingredients. After the intensity of federal agents and criminal conspiracies, the simple act of cooking felt like returning to solid ground.

"Brisket looks good," Jovie announced, examining the meat they'd put on the smoker at 5 AM. "Nice bark developing, internal temperature right on schedule."

"It's strange how normal this feels after everything that's happened," Lauren said, stirring a pot of beans while keeping one eye on the ribs she was preparing for the lunch rush.

"Normal is good," Melody observed from her station where she was precisely dicing onions. "Routine provides stability when external circumstances become unpredictable."

Jackie smiled at her niece's matter-of-fact wisdom. Even with federal protection and an ongoing murder investigation, they still had a restaurant to run and customers to feed. The community expected Charlie Joe's BBQ Shack to be open and maintaining that consistency felt important in ways that went beyond mere business obligations.

"Ladies, how are we doing this morning?" Tom Whitfield appeared at the back door, Blue at his side. "Thought I'd check in before I set up for the herding demonstration."

"Doing well," Jackie replied, though she noticed Tom's careful scan of the parking lot and the way he positioned himself to have clear sight lines in multiple directions. Word of federal involvement had clearly reached him.

"Any unusual visitors or phone calls since yesterday?" he asked quietly.

"A few reporters, but Jovie's been handling them," Lauren said. "Mostly people want to know when we'll be serving food again and whether the competition will be rescheduled."

"Competition's been postponed indefinitely," Tom said. "Martin Delgado announced it this morning. Said they need to review safety protocols before holding another event."

Jackie exchanged glances with Lauren. Safety protocols were probably code for figuring out which officials could be trusted after the corruption investigation became public.

"Tom," she said carefully, "has anyone approached you asking questions about our family or the restaurant?"

"Couple of strangers yesterday evening, claimed to be insurance investigators looking into liability issues related to the competition. Asked a lot of questions about your business practices, your experience with food safety, whether you'd ever had any violations or complaints."

"Insurance investigators?" Lauren asked skeptically.

"That's what they claimed. But they didn't know basic things that real insurance people would know, and they seemed more interested in finding problems than assessing actual risk."

Melody looked up from her onions. "What kinds of problems?"

"Financial irregularities, safety violations, anything that could be used to discredit your reputation or create legal troubles. I told them I didn't know anything about your business operations and suggested they contact your lawyer directly."

"Good," Jackie said. "That's exactly the right response."

As Tom settled into discussing security concerns, Melody found herself dicing onions with increasing intensity, her knife work becoming more precise and rapid. A sign Jackie had learned to recognize as stress management through controlled repetition.

"The corruption network has at least twelve confirmed participants across four states," Melody said, her voice carrying the tight quality it got when she was processing overwhelming information. "Multiple law enforcement jurisdictions, federal agencies, financial institutions. The interconnection patterns are exponentially more complex than anything we've dealt with before."

Blue, who had been sitting quietly beside Tom, suddenly rose and approached Melody's workstation with the deliberate, careful movement he used when assessing a situation that required his attention. He settled on the floor at her feet.

"Financial records show coordination between at least six different criminal enterprises," Melody continued, her dicing becoming even more methodical. "Sports betting, political corruption, agricultural commodity manipulation. The data correlation requirements alone..."

Blue paused beside her side, then gently pressed his head against Melody's leg. The same gesture he'd used during their first meeting. The contact was soft but deliberate, and Melody's rapid knife work immediately slowed.

"Oh," she said quietly, looking down at Blue with surprise. "Hello."

The dog settled beside her station, close enough that she could feel his calm presence without interfering with her work or contaminating the food. His intelligent eyes remained focused on her face, reading subtle signs of stress that even her family sometimes missed.

"He does that," Tom said gently. "Blue's got a sense for when someone's processing more than they can handle comfortably. Working dogs are bred to recognize when their partners are reaching their limits."

Melody moved away from the kitchen to the dining room, taking a seat. She found herself automatically stroking Blue's head, the repetitive motion providing a different kind of stress relief than her knife work. "The investigation complexity is... significant."

"But manageable," Jackie said, watching her niece's shoulders visibly relax as Blue pressed closer. "Especially when we have good partners helping us stay grounded."

"Statistical analysis suggests that emotional regulation during high-stress periods improves problem-solving efficiency by approximately thirty percent," Melody said, her voice already sounding more stable. "Blue appears to understand this principle intuitively."

Blue's tail wagged once, as if acknowledging the compliment, but he remained in position beside Melody. He was a calm, steady presence that seemed to anchor her while she continued processing the overwhelming scope of their investigation.

"Smart dog," Lauren observed, noting how naturally Melody had accepted the comfort. Her daughter rarely allowed anyone, human or animal, to interrupt her work routines, but Blue's presence seemed to enhance rather than disrupt her concentration.

As they continued their discussion about security and the postponed competition, Blue remained beside Melody, occasionally adjusting his position to maintain gentle contact with her arm or leg. The dog's intuitive understanding of neurodivergent stress responses was remarkable, providing exactly the right amount of calming pressure without overwhelming her sensory processing.

Once she was calm enough, she washed up and finished her dicing which was now its normal, efficient rhythm, and her voice carried none of the tension that had marked the beginning of their discussion.

"Thank you, Blue," she said quietly. "That was... helpful."

Blue's intelligent eyes seemed to convey understanding before he returned to Tom's side, his job of stress intervention complete.

As the morning progressed, their regular customers began arriving, and Jackie felt some of the tension of the past few days ease. Frank Kowalski came in for his usual sandwich and sweet tea and stayed to chat about the weather. Mrs. Rigby brought her book club for their weekly lunch meeting. Maria Santos arrived early for her shift, full of news about her youngest son's college acceptance.

"It's good to see everyone acting normally," Lauren said quietly as she prepared plates for the book club. "Makes it feel like maybe we can get through this without everything falling apart."

"Normal is relative," Jovie pointed out. "But yes, it's good to have familiar faces and regular routines. Helps balance all the craziness."

The lunch rush was busier than usual, partly because of curiosity about the murder investigation but mostly because word had spread that they were still serving excellent barbecue despite the surrounding drama. Jackie found herself taking genuine pleasure in watching customers enjoy their food, in the easy conversations with regulars, in the satisfaction of work well done.

"This is why Uncle Charlie Joe loved this place," she realized, watching Melody carefully explain the different sauce options to a first-time customer. "It's not just about the food. It's about being part of people's daily lives, providing something reliable and good in an uncertain world."

"Exactly," Lauren agreed, refilling sweet tea for a table of ranchers. "We're not just feeding people. We're maintaining community."

They were in the middle of the afternoon lull, cleaning equipment and prepping for dinner service, when Cassie Brennan walked through the front door. But this wasn't the bright, aggressive food blogger they'd met at the competition. This woman looked haggard, defensive, and angry.

"We need to talk," Cassie announced, approaching the counter where Jackie was updating inventory records.

"About what?" Jackie asked, maintaining a neutral tone despite the warning bells going off in her head.

"About the lies you've been spreading about me to the police and anyone else who'll listen." Cassie's voice was sharp with accusation. "I know you've been investigating me, trying to pin Tex Morrison's murder on me."

"We haven't been spreading lies about anyone," Lauren said calmly, moving closer to Jackie in a show of solidarity. "We've been trying to understand what happened to Tex."

"By accusing me of murder? By telling people I poisoned him because of some stupid restaurant review?" Cassie's composure was cracking, revealing something that looked like desperation underneath the anger.

Melody emerged from the kitchen, drying her hands on a towel, and positioned herself where she could observe Cassie's body language while staying close to the secure phone Agent Reeves had given them.

"No one has accused you of anything," Jackie said carefully. "We've simply been sharing information about the timeline of events at the competition."

"Information that makes me look guilty! Information that's destroying my reputation and my business!" Cassie's voice rose, causing other customers to look in their direction with concern.

"Cassie," Lauren said gently, "if you're innocent, then helping find the real killer should be in your best interest."

"I am innocent! But that doesn't matter when everyone's already decided I'm guilty because some bitter old man gave my restaurant a bad review!"

Jackie noticed several telling things about Cassie's outburst: she referred to Tex as a "bitter old man" despite claiming to respect his expertise, she seemed more concerned about her reputation than about justice for Tex, and she was displaying the kind of emotional volatility that suggested she was under significant stress.

"What exactly do you want from us?" Jackie asked.

"I want you to stop investigating me. I want you to tell the police that you were wrong about your suspicions. I want you to publicly state that I had nothing to do with Tex Morrison's death."

"We can't do that," Lauren said firmly. "We're not investigators. We're just concerned citizens who want to see justice done."

"Justice?" Cassie laughed bitterly. "This isn't about justice. This is about finding a convenient scapegoat so the real killers can get away with murder."

"What real killers?" Melody asked, her notebook ready to record anything significant.

"The people who were actually threatened by Tex's investigation into competition corruption. The people who had millions of dollars at stake, not just some food blogger trying to make a living."

Jackie felt a chill at Cassie's knowledge of the corruption investigation. "How do you know about Tex's investigation?"

"Because I was helping him," Cassie said, her voice dropping to an urgent whisper. "I was documenting evidence of judging irregularities, providing media coverage that would put pressure on corrupt officials, using my platform to expose the truth."

The revelation hung in the air like a bombshell. If Cassie was telling the truth, everything they'd assumed about her motive was wrong.

"You were working with Tex?" Lauren asked.

"For the past four months. He approached me after my review of the Central Texas Championship and questioned some suspicious scoring patterns. Said he needed someone with media credibility to help expose the corruption from the outside."

"Do you have proof of this?" Jackie asked.

Cassie pulled out her phone and showed them a series of text messages between her and a contact listed as "T.M." The messages discussed scoring anomalies, suspicious betting patterns, and coordination of media coverage for specific competitions.

"The last message I got from him was the night before he died," Cassie said, scrolling to show them. "'Tomorrow we gather final evidence. After Prairie Rose, we go public with everything.'"

Melody was studying the messages carefully. "These texts support your claim of cooperation with Tex Morrison, but they don't necessarily prove innocence. You could have killed him to prevent exposure of your own involvement in the corruption."

"I wasn't involved in the corruption! I was investigating it!" Cassie's frustration was evident. "And now because someone saw me near the judging tent, because I had access to the competition area, because Tex gave my restaurant a bad review, everyone assumes I'm the killer."

"The bad review gave you motive," Jackie pointed out. "And your behavior at the competition was suspicious."

"My behavior was investigative journalism! I was documenting everything, trying to identify the people who were manipulating results. Yes, I accessed areas I wasn't supposed to be in, but it was to gather evidence, not to commit murder."

"Evidence of what specifically?" Lauren asked.

"Photos of cash exchanges between competitors and judges, recordings of conversations about fixed results, documentation of betting patterns that indicated inside knowledge." Cassie's voice grew more urgent. "I have evidence that could expose the entire conspiracy, but no one will listen because they've already decided I'm guilty."

Jackie found herself facing a difficult decision. Cassie's story was plausible, and her evidence seemed genuine, but it could also be an elaborate deception designed to throw suspicion off herself.

"Cassie," she said finally, "if you really have evidence of corruption, you need to take it to the FBI. They're investigating this case now, and they have the resources to properly evaluate what you've discovered."

"The FBI?" Cassie looked startled. "This is a federal investigation now?"

"As of yesterday," Lauren confirmed. "They've been building a case against the corruption network for months."

Cassie was quiet for a moment, processing this information. "If the FBI is involved, then I'm either about to be vindicated or I'm in much more trouble than I realized."

"Which is it?" Melody asked directly.

"I guess we'll find out," Cassie replied. But her expression suggested she wasn't entirely confident in her own innocence, which made Jackie wonder what other secrets she might be hiding.

After Cassie left, promising to contact the FBI with her evidence, the three women sat in reflective silence.

"Do we believe her?" Lauren asked finally.

"Her story explains some of the inconsistencies in our timeline," Melody observed. "It also provides an alternative theory for her suspicious behavior at the competition."

"But it doesn't eliminate her as a suspect," Jackie added. "She could have been working with Tex and still killed him to protect her own involvement in the corruption or for completely different reasons."

"What do we tell Agent Reeves?" Lauren asked.

"Everything," Jackie said, reaching for the secure phone. "Let the professionals evaluate Cassie's claims and evidence. Our job is to provide information, not to determine guilt or innocence."

As she dialed the FBI number, Jackie reflected on how much more complicated their investigation had become. Just when they thought they understood the case, new information emerged that changed everything.

But that was often how real investigations worked with layers of truth and deception, competing motives and hidden alliances, the constant challenge of separating facts from assumptions.

Chapter Thirteen

Matt Klein arrived at the restaurant just as they were closing for the evening, his expression carrying the kind of serious concern that immediately put Jackie on alert. The retired FBI agent looked older than when she'd last seen him, and she could see the weight of worry in his eyes.

"Ladies," he said, settling at their usual corner table, "we need to talk. My contacts at the Bureau have been keeping me informed about your involvement in this investigation, and there are some things you need to know."

"Is this about Cassie Brennan's visit this afternoon?" Lauren asked, pouring Matt coffee from the pot they always kept ready for late conversations.

"Partly, but it's bigger than that." Matt opened a folder he'd brought with him. "Sarah Reeves is a good agent. I've worked with her before, but she may not have conveyed the full scope of what you're dealing with."

Melody looked up from the notebook where she'd been recording the day's events. "What scope?"

"This criminal organization didn't just start with barbecue competition manipulation," Matt said. "That's their most recent venture, but they've been operating for at least five years under different schemes. Sports betting, agricultural commodity fraud, even some political corruption in rural counties."

Jackie felt a familiar chill of recognition. "Like Uncle Charlie Joe's case?"

"Similar methodology, different target industries. They identify tight-knit communities where trust relationships are important, then systematically corrupt key figures to manipulate outcomes for profit." Matt pulled out several blurry photographs. "These are grainy and far away, but we think the same core group was behind a horse racing scandal in Kentucky, a cattle auction price-fixing scheme in Oklahoma, and now barbecue competition manipulation in Texas."

"How many people are we talking about?" Lauren asked.

"The inner circle appears to be three or four individuals with deep knowledge of rural community dynamics and the ability to blend into local cultures. But they recruit extensively from within each target community, so the total network could be dozens of people."

Melody was studying the photographs Matt had brought. "These don't look like typical criminal mugshots."

"How can you tell?" Jackie said, picking one up to examine it.

"Their clothing looks expensive and the way their posture looks," Melody said in her matter-of-fact tone.

"Because they're not criminals in the traditional sense. They're sophisticated con artists who specialize in corrupting legitimate businesses and social structures." Matt pointed to one photo showing a well-dressed man. "The suspected ringleader is Lou Paxton. I know his back is turned here. He's been connected to at least six different fraud schemes over the past decade, but he's never been successfully prosecuted."

"Why not?" Jackie asked.

"Because he's very good at staying in the background, letting his recruits take the legal risks while he controls the financial benefits. Plus, he has an unusual talent for identifying people who are vulnerable to corruption such as those with financial pressure, family problems, and career disappointments, then exploiting those vulnerabilities."

Lauren was studying another photograph showing a woman about her age with dark hair and sharp eyes. "Who's this?"

"Zoe Vonn, Paxton's lieutenant and the operational mastermind. She handles recruitment and day-to-day management of their various schemes. Very charming, very persuasive, and absolutely ruthless when crossed."

"Have either of these people been spotted in connection with the barbecue competitions?" Melody asked.

"That's what we're trying to determine. I'm guessing since you're asking, you didn't see them," Matt said. "They're experts at using aliases and staying out of official photographs, but someone matching Paxton's description was seen at two of the competitions where results appeared to be manipulated."

Matt closed the folder and leaned forward, his expression growing more serious. "Here's what concerns me about your situation. Tex Morrison wasn't just documenting corruption. He was close to identifying the leadership of the entire organization. His murder suggests they felt directly threatened."

"And now we're the ones investigating his death," Jackie said grimly.

"Exactly. Which makes you targets for the same people who killed him." Matt's voice carried the authority of decades in law enforcement. "Sarah Reeves mentioned that you've already been subjected to background investigations and legal intimidation tactics. That's their standard approach for dealing with problems."

"What comes after intimidation?" Lauren asked, though her tone suggested she didn't really want to know the answer.

"Direct action. They prefer to avoid violence because it draws law enforcement attention, but they won't hesitate to escalate if they feel cornered." Matt pulled out his phone. "I want to show you something that might change how seriously you take this threat."

The phone screen showed a news article from six months earlier: "Kentucky Horse Trainer Dies in Suspicious Accident." The article described how a man who had been asking questions about betting irregularities had died when his truck went off a rural road during what appeared to be ideal driving conditions.

"James Morrison," Matt said quietly. "Tex Morrison's younger brother. He was investigating suspicious betting patterns at Kentucky racetracks."

The room fell silent as the implications hit them.

"They killed Tex's brother?" Lauren asked in horror.

"We can't prove it, but the timing and circumstances are consistent with their pattern of eliminating threats. James had been gathering evidence of race fixing, and he died three days before he was supposed to meet with FBI agents."

"So, when Tex started investigating barbecue competition corruption..." Jackie began.

"He was continuing his brother's work, probably with his brother's murder as motivation," Matt concluded. "Which means his investigation was personal as well as professional."

Melody looked up from her notes. "That changes the dynamic significantly. Tex wasn't just a concerned judge, he was someone seeking justice for his family."

"And the killers knew it," Matt said. "Lou Paxton's organization doesn't like being challenged, especially by people who have personal stakes in exposing them."

Jackie felt the weight of inherited responsibility settling on her shoulders. "So, we're not just investigating Tex's murder. We're continuing a fight that's been going on for years."

"That's one way to look at it. Another way is to recognize that you're now in the same position James and Tex Morrison were in. You're gathering evidence against people who kill to protect their secrets."

The bluntness of Matt's warning hung in the air like a challenge. They could back away from the investigation, leave it to federal agents and hope for the best. Or they could continue their work, accepting the risks that came with confronting organized criminals.

"What would you do?" Lauren asked Matt directly.

"If I were still an active agent with federal backup and official authority? I'd pursue every lead and build the strongest case possible." Matt paused, meeting each of their eyes in turn. "If I were a civilian with family to protect? I'd seriously consider stepping back and letting the professionals handle it."

"But?" Jackie sensed there was more to his recommendation.

"But you're not typical civilians. You have unique access to the barbecue community, you've already identified crucial patterns that official investigators missed, and you have personal connections that make people trust you in ways they'd never trust federal agents." Matt's voice grew thoughtful. "Plus, if Lou Paxton's organization is planning to eliminate you as threats, backing down might not actually make you safer."

"What do you mean?" Melody asked.

"I mean they've already invested resources in researching your vulnerabilities and building cases against you. If they've decided you're dangerous to their operation, changing your behavior might not change their plans."

Jackie felt a familiar surge of stubborn determination. "So, we might as well keep investigating since they're going to target us anyway?"

"That's a decision only you can make. But if you do continue, you need to be much more careful about security, much more systematic about documenting everything, and much more aware of who you trust with information."

"Speaking of trust," Lauren said, "what do you think about Cassie Brennan's claims that she was working with Tex?"

Matt considered this carefully. "It's plausible. Using legitimate journalists to expose corruption is a common law enforcement strategy. But it's also possible that she's a very skilled liar trying to create reasonable doubt about her guilt."

"The FBI will be able to verify her story?" Jackie asked.

"They'll try, but Tex is dead and can't confirm her claims. They'll analyze her communications, check her financial records, interview people who might have witnessed their cooperation. But ultimately, her guilt or innocence might depend on evidence you haven't discovered yet."

"Such as?"

"Physical evidence from the crime scene, testimony from other participants in the corruption scheme, financial records that show payments or other connections to the criminal organization." Matt closed his folder. "The kind of evidence that often emerges only after suspects start making deals to avoid prosecution."

As Matt prepared to leave, he turned to Jackie. "You have my number. Call anytime. I'm available twenty-four hours. If anything happens that makes you feel unsafe, call me immediately. I may be retired from the Bureau, but I still have resources and contacts who can provide help."

"Thank you," Jackie said, genuinely touched by his continued concern for their family.

"Charlie Joe saved my life once, and I wasn't able to repay that debt before he died. Protecting his family is the least I can do to honor his memory."

After Matt left, the three women sat processing everything they'd learned.

"We're dealing with professional criminals who've killed at least two people to protect their operation," Lauren said finally.

"And we're apparently targets whether we continue investigating or not," Jackie added.

"But we also have federal protection, professional guidance, and unique advantages that could help solve this case," Melody concluded. "The question is whether the potential benefits outweigh the demonstrated risks."

Jackie looked around their small restaurant, thinking about Uncle Charlie Joe's legacy and Tex Morrison's murder and the Morrison brothers who'd died seeking justice. She thought about the community they'd built, the customers they served, and the principles Uncle Charlie Joe had taught them about standing up for what was right.

"I vote we continue," she said. "But we do it smart, we do it safe, and we do it together."

"Agreed," Lauren said immediately.

"Agreed," Melody added. "Though I suggest we implement additional security measures and communication protocols."

"Such as?"

"Check-in schedules, predetermined safe phrases for phone calls, backup meeting locations in case our usual places are compromised." Melody was already making notes. "Also enhanced documentation of all our findings and regular transmission of updates to Agent Reeves, Detective Sullivan, and Matt Klein."

Jackie felt pride in her niece's practical approach to a dangerous situation. Melody might be concerned about their safety, but she wasn't going to let fear prevent them from seeking justice.

"One more thing," she said as they prepared to head upstairs to their apartment. "From now on, we assume we're being watched and listened to. We be careful about what we discuss in public places, we vary our routines, and we trust our instincts if something feels wrong."

"Understood," Lauren said.

"And we remember that Uncle Charlie Joe and Tex Morrison both believed some things are worth fighting for, even when fighting is dangerous," Jackie added.

They were gathering their things when headlights swept across the restaurant windows. A familiar patrol car pulled into the parking lot, and Sheriff Martinez climbed out, moving with the casual stride of someone off duty rather than the focused urgency of official business.

"That's Ray," Lauren said. Jackie caught the note of pleased surprise in her sister's voice causing her to smile.

Ray knocked on the front door, and when Lauren opened it, he was holding a small bag from the hardware store and wearing civilian clothes, jeans and a flannel shirt that made him look younger and more approachable than his usual uniform.

"Evening, ladies," he said, touching his hat brim. "Hope I'm not intruding, but I wanted to check on your security setup after some of the information that's been coming to light about this case."

"Not intruding at all," Lauren said, stepping aside to let him in. "We were just finishing up for the night."

"Good timing then." Ray held up the hardware store bag. "I picked up some additional door and window locks, motion sensor lights for the parking area. Figured after what Matt Klein shared with Agent Reeves, you could use some extra security measures."

Jackie felt genuine gratitude for his thoughtfulness. "That's very considerate, Ray. We were just discussing security protocols."

"Mind if I take a look around, make some recommendations?" Ray asked. "Won't take long, and it would give me peace of mind knowing you're as protected as possible."

"Of course," Lauren said immediately.

Ray spent the next twenty minutes examining their current security setup, testing locks, checking sight lines, and making notes about potential vulnerabilities. His suggestions were practical and thorough. He suggested additional lighting for blind spots, better locks for the apartment entrance, and a simple alarm system that would alert them to anyone approaching the building at night.

"I can help install these tomorrow if you'd like," he offered. "It's my day off, and this kind of work is better done with two people anyway."

"We'd appreciate that," Jackie said. "Though we should probably pay you for your time and expertise."

"Absolutely not," Ray replied firmly. "This is about keeping my friends safe. That's not a billable service."

As Jackie and Melody headed upstairs to their apartment, Lauren walked Ray to his patrol car, enjoying the opportunity for a few minutes of conversation away from family and investigation pressures.

"Thank you for thinking of our security," she said as they reached his car. "It means a lot to know you're looking out for us."

"It means a lot to me to be able to help," Ray replied, leaning against the car door instead of immediately getting in. "Lauren, I have to ask, how are you handling all this? The investigation, the threats, the federal involvement. It's a lot for anyone to process."

"Some days better than others," Lauren admitted. "Today was harder after hearing about the Morrison brothers and realizing how dangerous this organization really is."

"I wish I could tell you the danger isn't real, but that would be dishonest." Ray's voice carried genuine concern. "These people have killed to protect their operation, and they won't hesitate to do it again if they feel threatened."

"Are you worried about us continuing to investigate?"

"Professionally, I think your insights have been valuable to the case. Personally..." Ray paused, clearly choosing his words carefully, brushing a stray hair from her face, "personally, I worry about the woman I'm falling for putting herself in danger."

The admission hung between them in the quiet evening air. Lauren felt her heart skip at his openness, at the way he'd made his feelings clear without demanding anything in return.

"The woman you're falling for?" she asked softly.

"If that's not presumptuous of me to say." Ray's voice carried a note of uncertainty that she found endearing. "I know we haven't known each other long, and I know the circumstances aren't ideal for starting something new..."

"Ray," Lauren interrupted gently, "the circumstances are what they are. But that doesn't change the fact that I'm falling for you too."

Ray's smile was visible even in the dim parking lot lighting. "Good. That's... that's very good."

They stood in comfortable silence for a moment, both processing the significance of what they'd just acknowledged. The evening air carried the scent of cooling barbecue smoke and the sound of crickets beginning their nightly chorus.

"When this investigation is over," Ray said finally, "I'd like to take you somewhere that has nothing to do with crime scenes or federal agents. Maybe dinner, again, somewhere quiet, where we can talk about normal things like favorite movies and childhood stories. We haven't done that in a while."

"I'd like that very much," Lauren replied. "Though I should warn you, my childhood stories involve a lot of family drama and sisterly conflicts."

"And I should warn you, my favorite movies tend toward old westerns and detective stories. Occupational hazard."

Lauren laughed. "I think we can work with that."

Ray opened his car door but paused before getting in. "Lauren, promise me something. If anything feels wrong, if you notice anyone watching the restaurant or asking unusual questions, if you get any sense that you're in danger, call me immediately. Day or night, on duty or off. Promise me."

"I promise," she said, touched by the protectiveness in his voice.

"And promise me you won't take unnecessary risks just to solve this case faster. Tex Morrison's murder will be solved, but not at the cost of your safety."

"I promise that too."

Ray started his car but rolled down the window before driving away. "See you tomorrow for the security installation. And Lauren? Thank you for letting me care about you."

As his taillights disappeared down the road, Lauren stood in the parking lot feeling a warmth that had nothing to do with the evening temperature. In the midst of investigation and danger, something beautiful was developing between them. Something that gave her hope for the future beyond the current crisis.

She found Jackie waiting at the top of the stairs to their apartment, wearing the expression of someone who'd been watching the entire interaction from the window.

"That looked like a significant conversation," Jackie observed.

"It was," Lauren said, unable to suppress her smile. "Ray's falling for me."

"And you're falling for him," Jackie replied. It wasn't a question.

"I am. Which is either terrible timing or perfect timing, depending on how you look at it."

"I'd say it's perfect timing," Melody said, emerging from her bedroom. "Statistical analysis shows that shared stressful experiences can accelerate emotional bonding and create stronger relationship foundations."

"Thank you for that romantic assessment," Lauren said dryly.

"You're welcome," Melody replied, missing the sarcasm entirely. "Also, Sheriff Martinez's security recommendations were very thorough. His personal investment in our safety is likely to result in better protection than standard law enforcement protocols would provide."

Jackie laughed. "She's not wrong. Having someone with both professional expertise and personal motivation looking out for us is definitely an advantage."

As they prepared for what they hoped would be their first peaceful night's sleep in days, Lauren reflected on how much her life had changed. Six months ago, she'd been focused solely on providing for Melody and managing their day-to-day survival.

Now she was part of a family business, involved in a federal investigation, there second one, and beginning what felt like the most promising romantic relationship she'd had in years.

Tomorrow would bring more challenges, more investigation, and more security concerns. But tonight, Lauren fell asleep thinking about Ray Martinez's promise to take her somewhere quiet when the danger was over, where they could talk about normal things and discover what lay ahead for them beyond crime scenes and federal agents.

It was a future worth looking forward to, and worth staying safe to reach.

Chapter Fourteen

The next morning, Melody found Aiden already at work in the restaurant's dining room when she came downstairs at 5 AM, his laptop open and papers spread across two tables in the same systematic organization style she used.

"You're here early," she observed, settling beside him with her coffee and notebook.

"Couldn't sleep. I walked over. Jovie let me in. I decided to work on cross-referencing the competition data with financial records," Aiden replied, then looked up at her with a slight smile. "Also, I was hoping to continue our conversation about forensic science programs."

Melody felt warmth spread through her chest. It was the same pleasant sensation she'd experienced during their dinner two nights ago. "Which aspect specifically?"

"The part where you mentioned considering graduate school. I've been researching programs that might interest you." He turned his laptop screen toward her, displaying a detailed comparison chart of forensic science programs across several universities. "I thought you might find the analytical approaches interesting."

A soft scratching at the back door interrupted their conversation, followed by Tom's quiet voice calling, "Blue, settle down. They're probably not even awake yet."

"Actually, we're up," Melody called back, rising to open the door.

Tom appeared with Blue at his side, the rancher looking slightly embarrassed. "Sorry to bother you so early. Blue heard voices and got insistent about checking on you. He's developed some strong opinions about your morning routine."

As if to prove Tom's point, Blue immediately crossed to Melody's table and settled beside her chair with the comfortable familiarity of a well-established habit. The dog arranged himself, so he was close enough to provide his calming presence without interfering with her work, then rested his head near her feet with a contented sigh.

"He does this every morning now?" Aiden asked, clearly charmed by the routine.

"Every morning since the federal investigation started," Tom confirmed, settling into a nearby chair with his own coffee. "Seems to think Melody needs supervision during these early work sessions. Won't settle until he's checked that she's calm and focused."

Melody found herself unconsciously reaching down to stroke Blue's head, the gesture having become as automatic as organizing her notebooks. "His presence improves my concentration efficiency during complex analysis tasks. The tactile input provides grounding when processing overwhelming data sets."

"In other words, Blue helps her think better," Tom translated with a fond smile. "Dogs have been working partners with humans for thousands of years. Blue just figured out that Melody's work is important and he wants to contribute."

Aiden was watching the interaction with professional interest. "There's documented evidence that animal-assisted therapy can significantly reduce cortisol levels and improve cognitive function, especially for individuals with heightened sensory processing. Blue seems to understand exactly what type of support Melody needs."

"He reads people like I read cattle," Tom said. "Been watching him work with Melody for a week or more now. He adjusts his approach based on her stress levels, provides exactly the right amount of contact without overwhelming her system."

Blue's tail thumped once against the floor, as if acknowledging the discussion, but he remained in his settled position beside Melody's chair. His presence had become such a natural part of her morning routine that she'd automatically arranged her papers and laptop to accommodate his space.

Tom left them to go talk with Jovie outside. "Just call if you need me."

For the next hour, they worked together in comfortable synchronization, sharing insights into the investigation while discussing academic possibilities. Melody found herself appreciating not just Aiden's intellectual contributions, but the way he remembered details from their personal conversations and followed up on them thoughtfully.

The dog remained quietly alert, occasionally shifting to maintain gentle contact with Melody's leg, providing steady grounding while she shared insights about the investigation and discussed academic possibilities with Aiden.

"Aiden," she said as Jackie and Lauren began arriving for morning prep, "thank you for researching those programs. Most people don't remember things I mention in passing."

"I remember everything you say," Aiden replied matter-of-factly. "You have interesting thoughts about most subjects."

"When do you go home?"

"I'm not sure. My father is happy about my friendship with you, so he said when I'm ready. Plus, we have this investigation that we are working on. I can't leave before we resolve it."

Melody understood his feelings about what the lack of closure would mean. It was like an itch you couldn't scratch.

Jackie and Lauren, who had come down just minutes earlier, exchanged knowing smiles as they went about their morning prep.

"They sure are cute together," she murmured to Lauren.

"They are. I'm happy for Melody to find a likeminded friend."

An hour later, with most of the morning prep done, Jackie was reviewing their security protocols over coffee when her phone rang. Agent Reeves calling earlier than usual meant something had changed.

"We've had a breakthrough," Reeves said without preamble. "Cassie Brennan's story checks out. We found corroborating evidence that she was indeed working with Tex Morrison to document the corruption."

"What kind of evidence?" Jackie asked, putting the call on speaker so Lauren could hear.

"Text messages recovered from Tex's personal phone, financial records showing payments to Cassie for what appear to be legitimate consulting services and photographs she provided that document cash exchanges between judges and unknown individuals at multiple competitions."

Lauren looked relieved. "So, she's not our killer?"

"She's still a person of interest because she had access and opportunity, but her motive has been eliminated. Which means we need to focus on who else wanted Tex Morrison dead badly enough to commit murder."

"The corruption ringleaders," Melody said immediately.

"Exactly. And Cassie's evidence has given us some new leads. We'd like you to review some photographs and see if you recognize anyone from the competition."

An hour later, Agent Reeves arrived at the restaurant with Detective Sullivan and a laptop full of surveillance images. They spread out at a corner table while Jovie and Maria handled the early lunch crowd.

"These are enhanced images from security cameras at three different competitions where results appear to have been manipulated. Better than the pictures that Matt brought you yesterday," Reeves explained, opening the laptop. "We're looking for anyone you might have seen at the Prairie Rose event."

The first few images showed crowds of competitors and spectators, too distant and blurry to identify specific individuals. But as Reeves scrolled through the photos, Jackie began to notice patterns. The same faces appearing at multiple events, always positioned where they could observe judging procedures or interact with officials.

"Stop," Melody said suddenly, pointing at the screen. "That man in the blue shirt. I've seen him before."

The image showed a middle-aged man with graying hair and wire-rimmed glasses, standing near a judging tent and appearing to have an intense conversation with someone whose back was to the camera.

"Where did you see him?" Detective Sullivan asked.

"At our competition, but not as a competitor or spectator. He was talking to Martin Delgado several times during the day, and I remember thinking it seemed like more than casual conversation."

Jackie studied the image more carefully. Even though he was casually dressed, she could see he was wearing expensive designer clothing. "He wasn't registered for anything official, but he acted like he belonged there. Always near the administrative areas, always watching the organization rather than the cooking."

"That's Lou Paxton," Agent Reeves said grimly. "The suspected ringleader Matt Klein told you about. If he was at your competition, that confirms this operation was being managed at the highest levels."

"He was there to oversee Tex Morrison's murder," Lauren realized.

"Most likely. Paxton doesn't usually involve himself directly in local operations unless something critical is at stake. Tex's investigation represented an existential threat to their entire network."

Reeves scrolled to the next image, showing a woman with dark hair in conversation with someone who looked like a competition volunteer. The trio recognized her from Matt's pictures.

"Zoe Vonn," she identified. "Paxton's lieutenant. Was she at your event?"

Melody consulted her notebook, flipping through her detailed observations from the competition day. "I don't think so, but there were a lot of people I didn't pay attention to. She could have been there without me noticing."

"What about him?" Detective Sullivan pointed to another image showing a man in his forties with a familiar profile.

Jackie felt recognition hit her like a physical blow. "That's Martin Delgado."

"You're sure?"

"Absolutely. But this photo shows him talking to Lou Paxton like they know each other well. At our competition, Martin acted like he was just the harried organizer trying to manage a difficult event."

Agent Reeves and Detective Sullivan exchanged significant glances.

"We've been investigating Martin Delgado for the past month," Reeves said. "Financial records show unexplained cash deposits coinciding with competitions where results appeared to be manipulated. We think he's been coordinating with Paxton's organization to ensure judging procedures could be compromised."

"So, Martin wasn't just the organizer," Lauren said slowly. "He was part of the criminal conspiracy."

"Which explains how the killers knew exactly when and how to access the judging area," Melody added. "Martin would have insider knowledge of all security procedures, volunteer schedules, and logistical vulnerabilities."

Jackie felt pieces of the puzzle clicking into place with disturbing clarity. "Martin came to our apartment the morning after

Tex died, supposedly because he was worried about being blamed for security failures. But really, he was trying to find out how much we suspected about the true cause of death."

"And when he realized we were actively investigating, he reported back to his handlers that we were becoming a problem," Lauren continued.

"That would explain the legal intimidation attempts and background research," Agent Reeves agreed. "Martin could have provided detailed information about your family's vulnerabilities."

Detective Sullivan was making notes as they talked. "We need to bring Martin Delgado in for questioning immediately. If he's been feeding information to the criminal organization, he might know details about their plans that could help us protect potential targets."

"Including us?" Jackie asked.

"Especially you. Martin knows your routines, your security measures, your family relationships. If Paxton's organization is planning direct action against you, Martin could have provided the intelligence they need."

The revelation that Martin Delgado was part of the conspiracy added a new layer of danger to their situation. He'd been in their apartment, had access to their investigation findings, and knew far more about their activities than they'd realized.

"Agent Reeves," Melody said carefully, "if Martin was working with the killers, does that mean our investigation has been compromised from the beginning?"

"Potentially, yes. Every time you shared information with Martin or discussed your findings where he might overhear, you were essentially reporting to the criminal organization." Reeves closed the laptop. "Which means they know exactly how much you've discovered and how close you are to exposing their operation."

"How close are we?" Lauren asked.

"Closer than they're comfortable with, obviously. We now have documented evidence of a criminal conspiracy involving competition manipulation, illegal gambling, and money laundering. We have photographs placing the ringleaders at crime scenes. We have a financial paper trail connecting multiple participants."

"But we still don't have proof of who physically administered the poison to Tex Morrison," Jackie pointed out.

"That's the final piece we need. Physical evidence or witness testimony that directly connects someone to the actual murder method." Detective Sullivan stood up, preparing to leave. "And we need to get it before the organization decides you're too dangerous to leave alone."

The federal agents gathered their things and left to arrest Martin Delgado. The sisters were left in the restaurant with enhanced security protocols and a new awareness of just how exposed their investigation had made them.

Jackie looked around the dining room so thankful for the afternoon lull. There weren't any customers to overhear their conversations.

The sound of a familiar vehicle pulling into the parking lot interrupted their planning. Through the window, they could see Sheriff Martinez's patrol car, and Ray himself climbing out with what appeared to be several bags from the hardware store.

"That's Ray," Lauren said, her face brightening despite their serious discussion. "He's here to install those security upgrades we talked about."

"Afternoon, ladies," he said, his gaze immediately finding Lauren with obvious warmth. "I've got everything we discussed for the security installation."

"Actually, the timing couldn't be better," Jackie said grimly. "We just learned that Martin Delgado has been working with the criminal organization all along."

Ray's expression immediately shifted to professional concern. "Martin's been feeding them information?"

"Everything. Our routines, our investigation methods, probably our security vulnerabilities," Lauren confirmed.

"Then these upgrades are even more important than we thought," Ray said, holding up the bags with renewed determination. "Motion sensor lights, upgraded locks, basic camera system for the entrances. Let's get you properly protected."

As Ray began unpacking equipment, Lauren moved naturally to assist him, their easy coordination evident in the way she anticipated what tools he needed and how he explained each security measure with patience clearly meant for her.

"This camera system connects to your smartphones," Ray explained, showing Lauren the app interface while standing close enough that their shoulders brushed. "You'll get alerts anytime someone approaches the building, day or night."

"And it works even if we're away from the restaurant?" Lauren asked, leaning in to see the screen better.

"Absolutely. The alerts follow you wherever you are." Ray's voice carried both technical explanation and personal concern. "Though I hope you won't need to be anywhere too dangerous while this investigation continues."

Their eyes met during the demonstration, and Jackie could see the way Ray's professional focus softened when he looked at Lauren, and how Lauren's usual efficiency became more graceful when Ray was nearby.

"These new locks are much more secure," Ray continued, working on the front door deadbolt while Lauren held his tools. "Hardened steel, anti-tamper mechanisms, much better than what you had before."

"You know a lot about security systems," Lauren observed, watching his competent installation work with obvious appreciation.

"Part of the job. Though I'll admit, I've never been quite so personally invested in making sure a security installation was perfect," Ray replied, glancing up at her with a smile that was both professional and intimate.

Twenty minutes later, Ray had installed motion sensors at both entrances and was testing the upgraded door locks with systematic thoroughness.

"There," he said, demonstrating the new deadbolt mechanism for Lauren. "Much better protection, and these locks are designed to resist the kind of tampering techniques criminals typically use."

"Thank you for prioritizing this," Lauren said, her gratitude evident. "Knowing Martin has been reporting our activities makes these upgrades feel essential rather than just precautionary."

"I'm always going to prioritize your safety," Ray replied quietly, his hand briefly covering hers as she tested the new lock. "All of you, but especially..."

"Especially Lauren," Melody finished from across the room. "Your romantic attachment creates heightened protective instincts. It's a predictable behavioral response."

Ray chuckled at Melody's clinical assessment while his cheeks reddened slightly. "Your daughter has a very direct way of analyzing situations."

"She's not wrong though," Lauren said, her smile warm and personal. "And I appreciate that your protective instincts come with actual useful skills like security installation."

As Ray packed up his tools, their conversation remained easy and comfortable despite the serious circumstances that had made the security upgrades necessary.

"Ray," Lauren said as he prepared to leave, "this investigation keeps getting more complicated, but having you looking out for us... it makes everything feel more manageable."

"That's what I'm here for," Ray replied, his voice carrying promise beyond just professional duty. "Whatever this investigation throws at us, we'll handle it together."

After Ray left, Jackie noticed Lauren's obvious contentment as she tested the new security features.

"He's really committed to keeping us safe," Jackie observed.

"He's committed to me," Lauren corrected with a soft smile. "The security measures are just one way he shows it."

"This definitely help keep us safer," Jackie said. "Martin. I can't believe it."

"Me either. He was working against us the whole time," Lauren said, watching Ray's car drive away. "He seemed so genuinely worried about Tex's death."

"Sociopaths are often excellent actors," Jackie replied grimly. "They can fake genuine emotion when it serves their purposes."

"The question now is what other information Martin provided to his handlers," Melody observed. "If he knows our security arrangements, our daily routines, our investigation methods, we may need to change everything."

Jackie was already thinking through the implications. "We need new communication protocols, different meeting places, varied schedules. And we need to assume that anything we discussed in Martin's presence has been reported to Lou Paxton."

"Including our theories about Cassie Brennan," Lauren realized. "If the real killers know we suspected her initially, they might have decided to frame her more thoroughly."

"Or they might have decided she knows too much about their operation and needs to be eliminated too," Melody said with characteristic directness.

The thought of Cassie Brennan as another potential target rather than a suspect changed Jackie's perspective on their responsibility. If they'd helped expose someone who was actually working against the criminal organization, they had an obligation to ensure her safety.

"We need to warn Cassie," she said, reaching for the secure phone Agent Reeves had provided. "If Martin reported our suspicions to his handlers, she could be in immediate danger."

But when Jackie tried calling the number Cassie had given them, it went straight to voicemail. Her attempts to reach Cassie through her blog and social media platforms also failed to get responses.

"Either she's being very careful about communication security," Lauren said, "or something's already happened to her."

The possibility that another person might have been killed because of their investigation filled Jackie with a sick sense of responsibility. They'd started this as a search for justice for Tex Morrison, but their efforts might have put additional people at risk.

"We need to find her," she said firmly. "If Cassie Brennan is in danger because of information we provided to Martin Delgado, we have an obligation to help protect her."

"How?" Melody asked practically.

"By finding her before Lou Paxton's people do," Jackie replied. "And by making sure the FBI has all the evidence they need to arrest everyone involved in this conspiracy before anyone else gets killed."

As they began planning their search for Cassie Brennan, Jackie realized their investigation had entered a new and more dangerous phase. They were no longer just seeking answers about a murder that had already occurred; they were racing to prevent additional killings.

As the adults discussed their search strategy, Aiden moved protectively closer to Melody, his concern evident in the way he positioned himself between her and the door.

"Maybe Melody should stay here," he suggested quietly. "If we're dealing with professional criminals who've already killed once..."

"I go where the investigation goes," Melody replied firmly, though she appreciated his protectiveness. "My analytical skills are needed for pattern recognition and timeline verification."

"Then I go with you," Aiden said immediately. "My forensic science background could be useful, and..." He paused, clearly debating whether to voice his personal motivations.

"And you want to keep me safe," Melody finished matter-of-factly.

"Yes. I know you're capable and intelligent and perfectly able to take care of yourself. But I also care about you too much to let you walk into danger without backup."

Melody felt a flutter of warmth at his confession. No one had ever cared about her safety in quite that way, not as someone fragile who needed protection, but as someone valuable who deserved care.

"Aiden," she said quietly, "when this investigation is over, would you like to discuss our future plans together? Academic programs we might both attend, research projects we could collaborate on, that sort of thing?"

His smile was brilliant. "I'd like that very much. I've been hoping you'd want to continue working together."

"Not just working together," Melody said with unusual boldness. "I think I'd like to continue everything together."

Lauren caught Melody's eye and smiled. Her worry about her daughter's future was no longer feeling as desperate as it once did. Perhaps Melody could find her way to people that supported her and would help take care of her. It warmed her mama's heart.

Chapter Fifteen

The search for Cassie Brennan began at her hotel, but the desk clerk at the Prairie Rose Inn informed them that she'd checked out early that morning without leaving a forwarding address.

"Paid in cash, seemed in a hurry," the clerk said, consulting his records. "Left around 6 AM, which was odd since she'd reserved the room through tonight."

Jackie exchanged worried glances with Lauren and Melody. Six AM was before Agent Reeves had confirmed Cassie's story, which meant she'd fled without knowing she'd been cleared as a suspect.

"Did she say where she was going?" Lauren asked.

"Just that she had an emergency back in Austin and needed to leave immediately. Asked about the fastest route to I-35."

Austin was a two-hour drive, which meant Cassie had a significant head start if that's where she was actually going. But Jackie's instincts suggested that someone running from potential murder charges might not head straight home where authorities could easily find them.

"We need to check her restaurant," Jackie said as they walked back to their car. "If she's really innocent and trying to prove it, she might have gone to gather evidence from her own business records."

Jovie and Maria had already agreed to run the restaurant while they looked for Cassie.

"Aiden, I think it best you stay here in Prairie Rose and be our eyes in town," Jackie said.

"But ..." he started to argue.

"I know you want to be with Melody. I understand, but if something happens, you need to provide everything we've found to the federal agents and the police. It is important."

He reluctantly agreed. Melody looked back as she climbed into the car peering through the back window until she couldn't see him any longer.

The drive to Austin took them through rolling Hill Country that reminded Jackie of the peaceful life they'd built in Prairie Rose. It seemed surreal to be chasing potential murder victims through the same landscape where they'd learned to smoke brisket and serve their community.

"There," Melody said, pointing to a small strip mall ahead. "Grillin' Dreams BBQ."

The restaurant looked closed despite the lunch hour, with no cars in the parking lot and a "Temporarily Closed" sign taped to the front door. But Jackie noticed that the sign appeared hastily made, as if it had been put up recently.

"Someone's been here," Lauren observed, pointing to fresh tire tracks made on the damp pavement of the parking lot. "Multiple vehicles, probably within the past few hours."

They walked around the building, looking for signs of recent activity. Behind the restaurant, they found Cassie's car parked near the dumpster, but when Jackie peered through the windows, it appeared empty.

"Her purse is still in the front seat," she said. "And her laptop bag. She wouldn't have gone far without those."

Melody was examining the back door of the restaurant. "This lock has been forced recently. See the fresh scratches around the deadbolt?"

Jackie felt her apprehension spike. "Someone broke in, probably after Cassie arrived. Question is whether she got away or whether we're too late."

"There are no other cars," Lauren said, looking around.

The back door was slightly ajar, which seemed ominous. Jackie pushed it open carefully, calling out, "Cassie? Are you here?"

No response, but they could hear faint sounds from inside the building. It might have been muffled voices or movement in the dining area, but it was hard to tell.

"We should call Agent Reeves," Lauren whispered.

"And wait twenty minutes, or longer if they are still back in Prairie Rose, for backup while something happens to Cassie?" Jackie replied. "We go in carefully, but we go in."

The kitchen was small and appeared to have been searched recently. Drawers were pulled out, papers scattered across prep surfaces, and several filing cabinets stood open with their contents partially removed.

"Someone was looking for something specific," Melody observed quietly. "This isn't random vandalism. It's systematic document retrieval."

They moved carefully and quietly toward the dining room, where the sounds they'd heard were becoming clearer. It was definitely voices, at least two people, and one of them sounded distressed.

"I told you, I don't have the originals here," a woman's voice said. It sounded like Cassie but strained with fear or pain. "Everything's in a safety deposit box in Dallas."

"Dallas is a long way to go based on the word of someone who's been lying to us for months," replied a man's voice that Jackie didn't recognize. "We think you have copies hidden somewhere in this restaurant."

"I don't! I swear I gave Tex everything I had. All my evidence is with the FBI now."

"The FBI doesn't have everything, or our source would have warned us. You kept backups, and we're going to find them."

Jackie motioned for Lauren and Melody to stay back while she crept closer to get a visual on the situation. Through the partially open kitchen door, she could see into the dining room where two men in dark clothes were standing over Cassie, who appeared to be tied to a chair.

One of the men matched the photograph Agent Reeves had shown them of Lou Paxton. The other was younger and had the alert posture of someone comfortable with violence. Neither had noticed Jackie's presence yet.

She retreated quietly to where Lauren and Melody waited.

"Two men, both armed, holding Cassie hostage," she whispered. "One is definitely Lou Paxton. They're looking for evidence they think she hid here."

"We call for backup now," Lauren said firmly.

"Agreed. But we also need to create a distraction to buy time." Jackie was already formulating a plan. "Melody, can you trigger the fire alarm system from back here?"

"Probably. Most commercial buildings have manual pull stations near the exits."

"Do it. Lauren, call 911 and Agent Reeves simultaneously. Tell them we have eyes on Lou Paxton holding a hostage at Grillin' Dreams BBQ in Austin."

"What are you going to do?" Lauren asked, concern evident in her voice.

"I'm going to make sure those two don't leave with Cassie before help arrives."

As Melody located the fire alarm and Lauren made the emergency calls, Jackie positioned herself where she could observe the dining room while staying hidden. The fire alarm would create confusion and hopefully prompt the kidnappers to make mistakes.

The piercing sound of the alarm filled the building, causing immediate chaos in the dining room.

"What the hell?" the younger man said, moving toward the windows to check for fire department response.

"It's a distraction," Paxton said calmly. "Someone's here. Find them."

Jackie realized her plan had backfire. Instead of creating an opportunity for escape, the alarm had alerted the criminals to their presence. Now they were trapped in the building with armed kidnappers who knew they were being watched.

"Kitchen," the younger man called out. "I heard something from the kitchen."

Jackie motioned urgently for Lauren and Melody to hide behind the large prep tables while she looked for anything that could serve as a weapon. The best she could find was a heavy cast-iron skillet, which would have to do.

The dining room door burst open, and the younger man entered with his gun drawn, scanning systematically for intruders. Jackie held her breath, pressed against the wall beside the industrial refrigerator.

"Nothing here," the man called back. "Must have been the alarm system malfunctioning."

But as he turned to leave, his foot kicked against Melody's notebook, which had fallen from her bag. He looked down, then up, his gaze finding their hiding spot behind the prep tables.

"Found them," he called out with grim satisfaction.

Jackie stepped out from behind the refrigerator, raising the skillet. "Let Cassie go and we'll walk away from this."

The man laughed. "Lady, you brought a frying pan to a gunfight. Not your smartest decision."

"Maybe not, but the Austin Police Department and FBI are already on their way," Jackie replied, trying to project more confidence than she felt. "You've got maybe five minutes before this place is surrounded."

"Then we better work fast," Lou Paxton said, appearing in the doorway with Cassie as a human shield. "You three are the family that's been causing us so much trouble. Perfect timing. We can eliminate all our problems at once."

Jackie felt cold dread settle in her stomach as she realized they'd walked into a trap. Instead of rescuing Cassie, they'd given the criminals exactly what they wanted with all their targets in one isolated location.

"You killed Tex Morrison," Lauren said, standing up from behind the prep table with her hands visible. "And his brother James."

"Business decisions," Paxton replied without emotion. "They were threats to a profitable operation. Just like you."

"The FBI knows who you are," Melody said, also emerging from hiding. "Killing us won't stop the investigation."

"But it will eliminate the witnesses who can connect us to specific crimes. Federal investigations are much harder to pursue when key sources of information are no longer available."

Jackie realized that Paxton was probably right. Their deaths would significantly hamper the federal case, even if it didn't stop it entirely. At least she'd thought to leave Aiden with all of their evidence, but she wasn't going to let that slip.

"However," Paxton continued, "we're reasonable people. If you agree to stop your investigation and forget what you've learned, we might be able to reach an accommodation."

"What kind of accommodation?" Jackie asked, though she didn't believe Paxton had any intention of letting them live.

"You return to your little restaurant and focus on serving barbecue. We disappear and never bother your community again. Everyone wins."

"Except Tex Morrison," Lauren said firmly. "He doesn't get justice."

"Tex Morrison got what happens to people who interfere in business that doesn't concern them. Same thing that happened to his brother, and the same thing that will happen to you if you don't accept our generous offer."

The sound of sirens in the distance interrupted Paxton's threat. Police response was faster than Jackie had expected, which meant they had maybe two minutes before the building would be surrounded.

"Looks like negotiation time is over," Paxton said, tightening his grip on Cassie. "We're leaving, and we're taking insurance policies to make sure we get away clean."

Jackie realized with growing horror that Paxton intended to use them as hostages to escape police custody. But as the sirens grew louder, she also realized they might have one chance to turn the tables.

"The fire alarm," she said quietly to Lauren. "When the first responders arrive, they'll expect to find people evacuating. If we can create enough confusion..."

"We run for the exit and hope the police can protect us," Lauren finished.

It wasn't much of a plan, but it was better than passively accepting their fate as hostages to desperate criminals.

As flashing lights appeared through the restaurant windows and authoritative voices began shouting commands outside, Jackie prepared to fight for their lives in whatever way presented itself.

The search for Cassie Brennan had become a fight for survival, and the outcome would determine not just their fate but the future of the federal investigation into the criminal organization that had already killed too many people.

Chapter Sixteen

The sound of car doors slamming and shouted commands from outside created a cacophony that seemed to energize Lou Paxton rather than worry him. Jackie watched his expression shift from annoyed impatience to calculating focus, and she realized with growing dread that he'd been in this kind of situation before.

"Austin PD, this is Lieutenant Kirkland," a voice called through a bullhorn. "We have the building surrounded. Send out any hostages and we can discuss terms."

Paxton smiled coldly. "They think this is a negotiation. That's their first mistake."

He nodded to his associate, who quickly moved to the restaurant's front windows and peered through the blinds. "At least six patrol cars, tactical van just arrived. They're setting up a perimeter but haven't moved to surround the back exit yet."

"Good. We stick to the plan." Paxton tightened his grip on Cassie, who looked pale but determined. "You four are going to help us walk out of here."

"We're not going to be your hostages," Lauren said firmly, stepping protectively closer to Melody.

"You already are," Paxton replied. "The only question is whether you cooperate and possibly survive, or resist and definitely don't."

Jackie felt her legal training kick in, analyzing their situation with the same systematic approach she'd used in complex negotiations. Paxton needed them alive to get past the police perimeter, which gave them some temporary value. But once he was clear of law enforcement, that value would disappear quickly.

"What's your exit strategy?" she asked, buying time while scanning the kitchen for anything that could help them.

"Simple. We walk out the back door with you as human shields, get to our vehicle, and drive away. The police won't risk shooting with innocent civilians in the line of fire."

"And then?"

"Then you become unnecessary complications that need to be resolved."

Melody, who had been unusually quiet, suddenly spoke up. "Your plan has several logistical flaws that significantly reduce your probability of success."

Paxton stared at her. "Excuse me?"

"Police tactical doctrine for hostage situations prioritizes containment over immediate resolution. They've had time to position snipers at multiple angles, block all vehicular exits from this parking area, and coordinate with federal agents who already have detailed intelligence about your organization." Melody's voice carried her usual matter-of-fact tone despite their desperate situation. "Your escape window closed approximately three minutes ago."

"She's right," Cassie said, speaking for the first time since they'd arrived. "I called the FBI before I came here. They've been tracking Lou Paxton's movements for weeks, waiting for him to make a mistake like this."

Paxton's confident demeanor cracked slightly. "You called them before you came here?"

"When I left Prairie Rose, I contacted Agent Reeves and told her I was coming to Austin to gather evidence from my restaurant. She offered federal protection, but I thought I could handle it alone." Cassie managed a weak smile. "Turns out I was wrong about that."

"So, the FBI knows we're here," the younger man said, anxiety creeping into his voice.

"They know, they're coordinated with local police, and they have detailed information about your criminal organization's structure and operations," Melody confirmed. "Statistically, your chances of successful escape are now less than three percent."

Jackie felt a spark of hope at Melody's analysis, but Paxton's response was swift and violent. He struck Cassie across the face with his free hand, causing her to cry out in pain.

"Shut up, all of you. We're leaving, and anyone who argues gets the same treatment."

But as Paxton prepared to move toward the back exit, the restaurant's front door exploded inward. Tactical officers in full gear poured through the entrance, moving with practiced efficiency.

"Federal agents! Drop your weapons!"

Instead of surrendering, Paxton's associate opened fire, sending the tactical team diving for cover behind overturned tables.

The deafening sound of gunshots in the enclosed space was overwhelming, and Jackie instinctively pushed Lauren and Melody toward the floor.

"Kitchen, now!" she shouted over the chaos.

They scrambled on hands and knees toward the relative safety of the industrial equipment while bullets shattered windows and punched holes in the dining room walls. Jackie could hear Paxton shouting orders to his associate, but the words were lost in the ongoing gunfire.

"Are you hit?" Lauren asked, checking Melody for injuries.

"No, but we need to get lower," Melody replied, pulling them behind the massive prep sink. "Ricochets are unpredictable in enclosed spaces."

The gunfire stopped abruptly, replaced by tense silence and the sound of someone reloading. Jackie risked a glance around the sink and saw that the tactical team had taken defensive positions but hadn't advanced into the dining room.

"We have civilians in here," someone called out. "Hold your fire unless you have a clear shot."

Jackie realized the police were constrained by their presence. They couldn't use overwhelming force while hostages were in the line of fire. Which meant the standoff could continue indefinitely unless something changed the dynamic.

"Cassie," she called out quietly. "Where are you?"

"Behind the counter," Cassie replied, her voice strained. "Paxton's using me as cover, but I think his partner's been hit."

Through the kitchen door, Jackie could see that the younger man was indeed wounded, clutching his shoulder while trying to maintain his position near the front windows. Blood was spreading across his shirt, and his movements were becoming less coordinated.

"Lou, we need to get out of here," the wounded man said. "I can't hold them off much longer."

"We're not leaving without our insurance," Paxton replied, but his voice carried less conviction than before.

"The insurance isn't worth dying for."

"It is if we want to avoid spending the rest of our lives in federal prison."

Jackie saw an opportunity in the dissension between the two criminals. If she could create enough distraction to separate Paxton from Cassie, the tactical team might have a clear shot.

"Lauren, when I give the signal, throw that pot as hard as you can toward the dining room," she whispered, pointing to a large stockpot within reach.

"What signal?"

"You'll know it when you see it."

Jackie took a deep breath, then stood up and walked toward the kitchen door with her hands visible.

"Mr. Paxton," she called out in her most authoritative courtroom voice. "I'm an attorney, and I'd like to discuss a possible resolution to this situation."

"Get back in the kitchen or I'll shoot you where you stand," Paxton replied.

"Shooting me won't improve your legal situation. But I might be able to help you negotiate a deal that keeps you out of the death penalty."

"I'm not interested in deals."

"You should be. Right now, you're facing murder charges, federal racketeering, and now kidnapping with a firearm. That's life without parole even if you surrender peacefully." Jackie moved closer, noting how Paxton had to turn slightly to keep her in sight while maintaining cover behind Cassie. "But if you release the hostages and surrender, I can help you work with federal prosecutors."

"You think I'm stupid enough to trust a lawyer who's been working against me?"

"I think you're smart enough to recognize when your situation has become untenable," Jackie replied. "Your partner's wounded, and you're surrounded by federal agents, and every minute you delay makes any potential deal less attractive to prosecutors."

She was now close enough to the dining room to see the full tactical situation. At least eight officers in various positions, all with clear lines of sight to the area where Paxton was holding Cassie. But none of them could take a shot without risking hitting either Cassie or Jackie herself.

"Last chance, Mr. Paxton. Release Cassie and we can end this without anyone else getting hurt."

"The only way this ends is with me walking out of here," Paxton replied. "And that means keeping my insurance policy."

"Now!" Jackie shouted, diving toward the floor.

Lauren's pot flew through the kitchen doorway, clattering loudly as it struck the dining room wall. In the split second of distraction as Paxton turned toward the sound, Cassie twisted away from his grip.

The tactical team's response was immediate and precise. Three shots fired simultaneously, and Lou Paxton crumpled to the floor without having the chance to return fire.

The sudden silence that followed was deafening after the chaos of gunfire and shouting. Jackie lay on the kitchen floor, her ears ringing, waiting for confirmation that the threat was over.

"Clear!" someone called out. "Suspects down, hostages secure!"

Paramedics rushed into the building as tactical officers secured the scene. Jackie watched as Cassie was helped to her feet, shaken but apparently uninjured. The wounded associate was receiving medical attention while being handcuffed. Lou Paxton's body was being examined by the medical examiner.

"Are you okay?" Agent Reeves appeared at Jackie's side, helping her to her feet.

"I think so. Is it over?"

"This part is over. Lou Paxton won't be threatening anyone else." Reeves looked around the destroyed restaurant. "But we still have Zoe Vonn and the rest of their organization to deal with. Paxton was the operational leader, but the network extends beyond just him."

As they gave statements to federal agents and Austin police, Jackie felt both relief and exhaustion. They'd survived a direct confrontation with the criminal organization, but the cost had been high. Cassie's restaurant was destroyed, they'd all been traumatized by the violence, and the broader investigation was still ongoing.

"What happens now?" Lauren asked as they prepared to leave the crime scene.

"Now we go home and try to process what we've been through," Jackie replied. "And we hope the federal investigation can wrap up the rest of Paxton's organization without requiring any more help from us."

But even as she said it, Jackie suspected their involvement in this case wasn't over yet. Zoe Vonn was still out there, along with an unknown number of other conspirators. And people who'd invested years building a criminal empire didn't usually give up just because their leader had been killed.

Uncle Charlie Joe had taught them that justice sometimes required courage and sacrifice. Today they'd provided both, but Jackie had a feeling the final resolution of Tex Morrison's murder was still ahead of them.

Chapter Seventeen

The drive back to Prairie Rose felt longer than usual, weighted with the aftermath of violence and the sobering realization of how close they'd come to not making it home at all. Jackie kept glancing in the rearview mirror, checking for vehicles that might be following them, a paranoia that she knew would take time to fade.

"My ears are still ringing," Lauren said quietly, touching the side of her head. "I can't believe we were in an actual shootout."

"Statistically, most civilians never experience firearms violence directly," Melody observed from the backseat, but her voice lacked its usual clinical detachment. "The psychological impact can be significant even when physical injury doesn't occur."

Jackie reached over and squeezed Lauren's hand. "We survived. We helped save Cassie's life. And we eliminated a major threat to our community."

"But at what cost?" Lauren asked. "I keep thinking about what could have happened if the police had been five minutes later, or if Paxton had decided killing hostages was worth more than using them for escape."

"But they did and we made it," Jackie said with a confidence she wasn't exactly feeling herself right now.

The conversation was interrupted by Jackie's phone ringing. Agent Reeves calling for a status update.

"We're about thirty minutes from Prairie Rose," Jackie reported. "Physically okay, mentally processing."

"Good. I wanted to give you an update on what we learned from the Austin operation. Lou Paxton's death has already triggered significant activity within his network."

"What kind of activity?" Jackie asked, putting the call on speaker.

"Communications intercepts show increased coordination between remaining members, financial transfers suggesting they're trying to liquidate assets quickly, and intelligence indicating Zoe Vonn has taken operational control of what's left of the organization."

"Meaning?"

"Meaning she's likely to be more aggressive than Paxton was about eliminating perceived threats. Paxton preferred intimidation and legal manipulation. Vonn has a history of more direct solutions to problems."

Lauren leaned toward the phone. "Are we still in danger?"

"Potentially, yes. But we've also significantly weakened their organization and limited their resources. Plus, we now have multiple federal agencies coordinating to track down the remaining members."

"What do you need from us?" Jackie asked.

"Rest, recover, and stay alert. We may need you to identify suspects or provide testimony as we build cases against the remaining conspirators. But your active investigation phase is over. Let us handle the rest."

After Agent Reeves hung up, they drove the remaining distance in silence. As they crested the hill overlooking Prairie Rose, Jackie felt a wave of relief at seeing the familiar landscape and the restaurant sign in the distance.

"Home," Lauren said simply, echoing Jackie's thoughts.

But as they pulled into the restaurant parking lot, they were surprised to see Sheriff Martinez's patrol car already there, parked at an angle that suggested he'd arrived in a hurry. Ray himself was pacing on the front porch, his usually composed demeanor replaced by obvious agitation.

"Ray?" Lauren called out as they climbed from the car. "What are you doing here?"

Ray turned at the sound of her voice, and Lauren was struck by the relief that flooded his features when he saw them. He strode quickly across the parking lot, his official composure cracking as he reached them.

"Thank God you're all right," he said, his voice tight with emotion. "When Agent Reeves called to tell me about the Austin situation, about the shootout..." He paused, running a hand through his hair. "I've been here for an hour, waiting and trying not to imagine the worst."

Lauren felt her heart constrict at the raw worry in his voice. "Ray, I'm sorry. I should have called to tell you, but we're okay. Shaken up, but okay."

"You were held at gunpoint by professional criminals," Ray said, his voice carrying both relief and residual fear. "You were in a building where people were shooting at federal agents. 'Okay' is relative."

Jackie watched the interaction with interest, noting how Ray's professional training warred with his personal emotions. He was clearly struggling to maintain his sheriff's composure while dealing with the fear of losing someone he cared about.

"We were careful," Lauren said, stepping closer to him. "We had federal protection, and we followed all the safety protocols."

"Safety protocols don't stop bullets," Ray replied, his voice rough with emotion. "When I heard there had been gunfire, that civilians were involved..." He stopped, clearly trying to regain his professional control.

"But we're here," Lauren said gently, reaching out to touch his arm. "We're safe, and we're home."

Ray looked down at her hand on his arm, then back up at her face. "Lauren, I need to tell you something, and I need to tell you now because I realized today that I might not get another chance."

"Ray —"

"I'm falling in love with you," he said, the words coming out in a rush. "I know it's fast, I know the timing is complicated with the investigation, but when I thought about the possibility of losing you before I'd told you how I feel..." He shook his head. "I couldn't live with that regret."

Lauren felt tears prick her eyes at the honesty and vulnerability in his voice. "Ray, I'm falling for you too."

The relief on his face was immediate and profound. "Good. That's... that's good."

Jackie cleared her throat gently. "Maybe we should take this conversation inside? The parking lot isn't exactly private."

Ray seemed to remember where they were and stepped back slightly, his professional demeanor reasserting itself. But his hand found Lauren's and held it firmly as they walked toward the restaurant.

"I got a preliminary briefing from Agent Reeves about what happened in Austin," Ray said as they settled at their usual corner table. "Lou Paxton is dead, his associate is in custody, and Cassie Brennan is safe. But Zoe Vonn is still out there."

"Agent Reeves said she's taken control of what's left of the organization," Melody said.

"Which could make her more dangerous than Paxton was. Desperate leaders make desperate decisions." Ray's attention focused on Lauren. "I want to increase security around the restaurant. More frequent patrols, maybe a deputy stationed here overnight."

"Is that really necessary?" Jackie asked.

"After what happened today? Yes. Zoe Vonn knows you've been instrumental in dismantling her operation. She might decide that eliminating you is worth the risk."

Lauren squeezed Ray's hand. "What are you thinking?"

"I'm thinking I want you somewhere safe until this is over. All of you, but especially..." He paused, clearly aware that his personal feelings were influencing his professional recommendations.

"Especially me," Lauren finished. "Because of how you feel about me."

"Yes," Ray said simply. "I can't be objective about your safety anymore, Lauren. My judgment is compromised because my feelings are involved."

"That doesn't make your recommendations wrong," Jackie observed. "If anything, personal motivation might make you more thorough about security measures."

"Maybe. But it also means I need backup from other officers who can think clearly about tactical situations." Ray pulled out his phone. "I'm calling in additional resources. Federal agents, state police, whatever it takes to make sure you're protected."

"Ray," Lauren said gently, "we appreciate the concern, but we can't live under armed guard indefinitely."

"You can until Zoe Vonn is caught or eliminated as a threat."

The firmness in his voice brooked no argument, and Lauren found herself both touched by his protectiveness and slightly overwhelmed by the intensity of his concern.

"What about the restaurant?" she asked. "We have customers, employees, a business to run."

"We figure out a way to maintain operations while keeping you safe. Maybe increase staff so you're never alone, maybe modify hours so you're not here during vulnerable times." Ray was already working through logistics. "The important thing is that you stay alive to run the business long-term."

Jovie came in the back door as they were discussing security protocols, and her relief at seeing them safe was evident.

"Thank the Lord you're all right," she said, hugging each of them in turn. "The news reports made it sound like a war zone."

"It felt like one," Jackie admitted. "But Lou Paxton won't be threatening anyone anymore."

"And the rest of his organization?"

"Still out there, but we're not dealing with them directly anymore," Ray said firmly. "Federal agents are handling the rest of the investigation."

As evening settled over Prairie Rose and the enhanced security measures Ray had arranged took effect, Lauren found herself on the restaurant's back porch with Ray, watching the last of the sunset paint the Hill Country in shades of gold and orange.

"Are you really okay?" he asked quietly, studying her face in the fading light.

"I'm processing," Lauren admitted. "It's surreal, going from serving barbecue to being held at gunpoint to coming home and talking about normal things like security measures and employee schedules."

"Trauma can manifest in different ways, even when you think you're handling things well," Ray said. "If you start having trouble sleeping, or flashbacks, or anxiety about being in public places, that's normal and treatable."

"Is that your professional opinion or personal concern talking?"

"Both. I've seen enough people go through traumatic experiences to recognize the patterns. And I care about you enough to want to make sure you get whatever help you need to process what happened today."

Lauren leaned against the porch railing, feeling the weight of the day's events settling into her bones. "Ray, what happens when this is all over? When Zoe Vonn is caught and the investigation is closed?"

"What do you mean?"

"I mean, will what we have survive normal life? Right now, we're bonded by danger and adrenaline and shared concern. But what about when things are peaceful and ordinary?"

Ray was quiet for a moment, considering her question seriously. "I think what we have goes deeper than crisis bonding," he said finally. "I think I fell for your strength and your kindness and your dedication to your family long before this case. Those qualities don't disappear when the danger passes."

"And I fell for your integrity and your protectiveness and the way you balance professional duty with personal care," Lauren replied. "But I've never had a relationship that started under such intense circumstances."

"It started before this, but either way, we'll figure it out together, day by day, without the pressure of life-or-death situations to accelerate everything."

Lauren smiled at the simple reasonableness of his approach. "That sounds like a good plan."

Ray moved closer, his hand finding hers on the porch railing. "Lauren, I meant what I said earlier. I love you. Not just the idea of you, not just the excitement of danger and investigation. I love who you are, how you think, the life you've built with your family."

"I love you too," Lauren said, the words feeling both natural and momentous. "And I love that you care enough about my safety to call in reinforcements and modify your professional protocols."

"I'll always put your safety first," Ray said. "That's not going to change when this investigation is over. I'd like to kiss you, if that's okay."

"I'd like that." She smiled.

Ray's lips met hers in a kiss that was gentle and urgent at the same time, filled with all the emotion and promise they'd been building toward for weeks or longer. Lauren felt herself melting into his embrace, her hands fisting in his tactical vest as she kissed him back with equal intensity.

When they finally broke apart, both were breathing hard. Smiling sweetly at each other before they kissed again, more softly this time. This kiss held a promise of a future together. Whatever that meant for them, they both knew they wanted that.

As they stood together on the porch, surrounded by the peaceful sounds of evening in the Hill Country, Lauren felt a deep sense of gratitude for the unexpected gift that had emerged from their dangerous investigation. Finding love in the midst of crisis wasn't something she'd planned or expected, but it felt right in ways that defied logic or timing.

"What do you say we go inside and help Jackie and Melody process their own experiences from today?" Ray suggested. "Then maybe we can all get some rest, knowing that you're as safe as I can possibly make you."

"That sounds perfect," Lauren said, standing on her tiptoes to kiss him softly. "Thank you for caring about me enough to worry, and for being here when we got home."

"Thank you for coming home safe," Ray replied. "I don't know what I would have done if something had happened to you today."

As they rejoined Jackie and Melody inside the restaurant, Lauren felt a sense of completeness that had nothing to do with the investigation or the danger they'd faced. She'd found not just love, but the kind of partnership that could weather both crisis and calm, both professional challenges and personal growth.

Uncle Charlie Joe had brought them together as a family, but he'd also given them the foundation to build relationships that extended beyond blood ties. Ray Martinez had become part of that extended family, and Lauren looked forward to discovering what their future would hold once the immediate dangers had passed.

For now, it was enough to be home, to be safe, and to be loved by someone who understood the balance between protection and freedom, between professional duty and personal commitment.

Tomorrow would bring new challenges and continued threats from Zoe Vonn. But tonight, Lauren fell asleep knowing that Ray Martinez loved her enough to rearrange his professional priorities to keep her safe, and that she loved him enough to trust him with both her safety and her heart.

Chapter Eighteen

The next morning started like every other morning since they'd arrived in Prairie Rose. Too early but perfectly. Jackie started the smoker while Lauren started selecting and trimming their briskets to start. Once all the meat was smoking, they moved into the kitchen to begin sides.

Jovie arrived shortly after and began pouring coffee for everyone, her movements carrying the nervous energy of someone who'd been waiting for bad news. "I've been thinking about everything that's happened yesterday, and I need to tell you something important. It had slipped my mind because y'all had gone through so much."

Jackie felt her attention sharpen. "What?"

"Three days ago, a woman came by asking questions about your family. Said she was a reporter, but something about her didn't feel right. Asked too many personal questions, wanted to know about your security routines, whether you had any enemies."

"What did she look like?" Lauren asked.

"Late forties, dark hair, very polished appearance. Expensive clothes, confident manner, but her questions were more like interrogation than journalism."

Jackie and Lauren exchanged glances. The description matched the photographs they'd seen of Zoe Vonn.

"Did she give you a name?"

"Zelda Vann, but when I asked for her press credentials, she said she'd left them in her car and would come back with them later. Never saw her again."

"Zelda Vann. Close to Zoe Vonn," Melody noted. "She was conducting reconnaissance, probably planning some kind of action against us."

"But now that Paxton's dead, her priorities may have changed," Jackie said. "She might be more focused on escape and asset protection than revenge."

"Or she might be more motivated than ever to eliminate the people who destroyed her organization," Lauren countered.

They were discussing security precautions when Tom Whitfield appeared at the back door, Blue at his side and an expression of grim concern on his weathered face.

"Ladies, we need to talk. I've been keeping watch since I heard about the Austin situation last night, and there's been unusual activity around your property."

"What kind of activity?" Jackie asked, immediately alert.

"Vehicle parked on the ridge road for several hours yesterday, positioned where they could observe the restaurant with binoculars. Different car this morning, but same pattern. Someone's conducting surveillance."

"Could be federal agents providing protection," Lauren suggested hopefully.

"Federal agents would have identified themselves to me when I approached. These folks drove off as soon as they saw me coming." Tom settled into a chair, his expression serious. "I think Zoe Vonn is still out there, and I think she's planning something."

As if summoned by his words, Jackie's phone buzzed with a text from an unknown number:

Lou made his choice. Now you get to make yours. Midnight tonight, Charlie Joe's grave. You and your family meet me there. No police or more people die.

The message was followed by a photograph showing the exterior of Prairie Rose Elementary School with children playing in the schoolyard.

"She's threatening kids now," Lauren said, her voice tight with anger and fear.

"She wants to draw us out where she can control the situation," Jackie realized. "Away from federal protection, away from witnesses."

"It's a trap," Melody said simply.

"Obviously. But it's a trap we might have to walk into if she's really planning to hurt innocent people."

Tom was studying the message over Jackie's shoulder. "Charlie Joe's buried in Prairie Rose Cemetery, about two miles from here. Isolated location, multiple escape routes, good sight lines for an ambush."

"We call Agent Reeves immediately," Lauren said.

"Absolutely. But we also need to consider that Zoe Vonn has been planning this for days, maybe weeks. She'll have contingencies for federal involvement."

As Jackie called Agent Reeves to report the threat, she found herself thinking about Uncle Charlie Joe's final resting place. He'd chosen a simple grave in the town cemetery, surrounded by the community he'd served for thirty years. It seemed wrong that his peaceful rest would be disturbed by the violence of criminal revenge.

"Agent Reeves is coordinating with local and federal tactical teams," Jackie reported after ending the call. "But she agrees that Zoe Vonn probably has backup plans for official law enforcement response."

"So, what do we do?" Lauren asked.

"We do what Uncle Charlie Joe would do," Jackie said quietly. "We protect our community first, our family second, and ourselves last."

"Meaning?"

"Meaning we meet Zoe Vonn tonight, but we do it smart and we do it with backup she doesn't know about, just as we have been trying to do all along."

As if summoned by their planning, Matt Klein appeared at the restaurant's back door, his expression carrying the focused intensity of someone preparing for a dangerous operation.

"I heard about the threat," he said without preamble, settling at their usual corner table.

"Word travels fast."

"Yeah, Agent Reeves called me immediately knowing my relationship with you. She briefed me on the cemetery confrontation and thought I could provide tactical advice to you before tonight."

"We're listening," Jackie said, grateful for his expertise.

"Zoe Vonn is desperate, which makes her both more dangerous and more prone to mistakes," Matt began, opening a folder he'd brought. "She's lost her organization, her leadership, and probably most of her financial resources. This confrontation isn't just about revenge. It's about salvaging something from a completely failed operation."

"What does that mean for us?" Lauren asked.

"It means she'll try to control every aspect of the meeting. She'll want to dictate terms, manipulate the conversation, and create confusion that works to her advantage." Matt looked directly at Jackie. "But you have something she doesn't expect. Your legal training."

Jackie felt a spark of recognition. "You want me to treat this like a negotiation."

"Exactly. Zoe thinks she's dealing with amateur investigators who stumbled into her operation by accident. She doesn't know you're an experienced attorney who's spent years managing hostile negotiations and controlling difficult conversations."

"What's my approach?"

"Use your courtroom skills. Ask questions that force her to reveal information. Control the pace of the conversation. Make her defend her position instead of just making threats." Matt's voice grew more serious. "And remember, everything she says will likely be recorded by federal surveillance. Treat it like you're building a case, because you are."

Lauren looked between them. "Is this really going to be a negotiation, or is it going to be violence?"

"If done it right, it'll be both," Matt replied honestly. "She'll try to negotiate from a position of strength, but when she realizes she's actually trapped, she'll probably resort to violence. That's when federal agents move in."

"So, I keep her talking until the trap is sprung," Jackie said, understanding her role.

"Keep her talking, keep her revealing information, and most importantly, keep her focused on you instead of looking for the backup she can't see," Matt confirmed. "Your legal skills like reading people, controlling conversations, staying calm under pressure, are exactly what we need for this operation."

Jackie felt the familiar confidence that came with understanding her role in a complex situation. This wasn't just about confronting a criminal. It was about using every skill she'd developed as an attorney to protect her family and community.

"Any other advice?" she asked.

"Trust your instincts. If something feels wrong, if Zoe deviates from expected behavior, if the situation starts to spiral, signal for immediate extraction. Federal agents will be positioned to move at the first sign of real danger."

As Matt prepared to leave, he paused at the door. "Jackie, you've spent your career advocating for clients in difficult situations. Tonight, you're advocating for your family, your community, and justice for Tex Morrison. Use everything you've learned."

After Matt left, Jackie felt a sense of clarity about the confrontation ahead. This wasn't just about survival, but about using her professional skills to help law enforcement capture a dangerous criminal while protecting everyone she cared about.

The final confrontation was coming, but they would meet it together, with the support of their community and the resources of federal law enforcement.

Zoe Vonn had made a mistake in threatening innocent children. That threat had transformed their investigation from a search for justice into a fight to protect everything they cared about.

And when it came to protecting family and community, the Rodriguez women didn't back down.

Chapter Nineteen

Lou Paxton's death had ended one chapter of their investigation, but the knowledge that Zoe Vonn remained at large cast a shadow over what should have been relief. Agent Reeves had arrived just before their evening rush to review security protocols with Agent Reeves.

As Jackie was huddled with Agent Reeves discussing the coming night's confrontation, the restaurant's front door opened with more force than necessary. They looked up to see Wade Brooks entering, his usual aggressive confidence replaced by something that looked almost like vulnerability.

"Wade," Jackie said carefully, uncertain whether his presence represented a threat or merely another complicated conversation.

"I heard about what happened in Austin," Wade said without preamble, his voice carrying none of the hostility that had marked their previous encounters. "About Lou Paxton and the real criminals behind Tex Morrison's murder."

"News travels fast in small communities," Lauren observed, joining them from the kitchen where she'd been helping Jovie with morning prep.

Wade looked around the restaurant taking in the family photos on the walls, the evidence of community connection and genuine success that had nothing to do with criminal activity or corruption. His expression carried what appeared to be genuine shame.

"I owe you an apology," he said finally. "A big one. I've been bitter and suspicious and probably made your investigation harder when I should have been supporting neighbors."

"Wade, you couldn't have known —" Jackie began.

"Yes, I could have," Wade interrupted, his voice gaining strength. "I could have looked past my own jealousy and resentment long enough to see what was really happening. Instead, I was so focused on nursing old grudges that I missed the fact that real criminals were operating in our community."

Melody emerged from the back office where she'd been updating her investigation files, her notebook in hand as always. She studied Wade with the same analytical attention she applied to everything else, but her expression seemed less wary than it had during their restaurant visit.

"Your behavioral indicators during our previous meeting suggested genuine animosity toward the victim," she observed matter-of-factly. "But statistical analysis now indicates those emotions were based on professional grievances rather than homicidal intent."

"She's right," Wade said, managing a slight smile at Melody's clinical assessment. "I hated Tex Morrison's judging style, hated what I saw as bias against traditional barbecue methods. But I never would have hurt him. I'm not that kind of person, no matter how bitter I might have sounded."

"What about your comments about Tex 'getting what was coming to him'?" Lauren asked. "That seemed pretty hostile."

Wade's face flushed with embarrassment. "That was anger talking, not planning. I thought his death was some kind of cosmic justice for the way he'd treated traditional pitmasters. I didn't realize someone had actually murdered him, and I sure didn't think it was part of some organized criminal conspiracy."

Jackie studied Wade's body language, applying the same analytical skills she'd used in countless depositions and plea negotiations. His posture was open rather than defensive, his eye contact steady, his voice carrying genuine remorse rather than calculated manipulation.

"You really didn't know about the corruption network?" she asked.

"I didn't even know there was a corruption network," Wade replied. "I thought competition judging was just subjective bias and personal preferences. The idea that results were being systematically manipulated for gambling and money laundering... that never occurred to me."

"But you were arguing with Martin Delgado throughout the competition," Melody pointed out, consulting her notes. "Multiple heated conversations, apparent disputes about procedures..."

Wade sighed deeply. "Martin owed me money from a catering job last year. Three thousand dollars for a wedding that he helped organize but never paid me for. I kept trying to get him to settle up, and he kept making excuses. That's what we were arguing about, unpaid invoices, not murder plots."

The explanation was so mundane, so typical of small business disputes, that it immediately rang true to Jackie. She'd handled dozens of similar cases during her legal career.

"And you were away from your cooking station during the critical time period because...?" Lauren asked.

"Because I followed Martin to the parking lot to demand payment," Wade admitted. "I was tired of being put off, tired of him avoiding my calls. I cornered him out there and told him I wasn't leaving until he gave me a timeline for payment. He headed back towards the judging area, so I followed him there. Probably not my finest moment as a competitor."

"Statistical probability supports this explanation," Melody said, making notes. "Financial disputes between small business owners represent common source of public disagreements, significantly more probable than coordinated criminal activity."

Wade looked between the three women with something approaching gratitude. "You've been more generous about this than I deserve. I know how suspicious I must have looked, how hostile I was during your visit to my restaurant."

"You were protecting what you'd built," Jackie said, her lawyer's instincts recognizing the truth when she heard it. "Twenty-three years of work, watching other restaurants succeed while yours struggled. That kind of pressure can make anyone defensive."

"It doesn't excuse the way I treated you," Wade replied. "Charlie Joe built something good in Prairie Rose. You've honored that legacy and contributed to this community in ways I was too bitter to recognize."

Lauren poured Wade a cup of coffee without being asked, a gesture that seemed to surprise him with its simple kindness. "Apology accepted. We've all been under pressure during this investigation."

"The real question now is what happens next," Jackie said. "Zoe Vonn is still out there, and she's probably desperate enough to be dangerous. We need to focus on staying safe and helping law enforcement finish what they started."

Wade straightened, his expression becoming more determined. "If there's anything I can do to help; such as, surveillance, extra security, someone to watch your back, just ask. I know I can't undo the suspicion and hostility, but I'd like to try to make things right."

"Actually," Melody said, looking up from her notebook, "your restaurant's location provides excellent sight lines to several approach routes to Prairie Rose. If Zoe Vonn attempts to enter the area, you might be positioned to provide early warning."

"Consider it done," Wade said immediately. "I'll keep watch and report anything suspicious. It's the least I can do after making your lives more difficult when you were trying to solve a murder."

As Wade prepared to leave, he paused at the door and looked back at them. "Charlie Joe was right about family. About building something that matters more than competition or profit. I'm sorry it took me so long to see that."

After he left, the three women sat in thoughtful silence, processing another resolution in their complex investigation.

"Well," Lauren said finally, "that eliminates our prime suspect and gives us an ally we didn't expect."

"It also demonstrates the difference between petty local rivalry and actual criminal behavior," Melody observed. "Wade Brooks represents normal community conflict resolution, not homicidal intent."

Jackie nodded, feeling both relief and renewed focus. "Which means our attention needs to shift entirely to Zoe Vonn. She's the real danger now, and she's had time to plan whatever revenge she thinks we deserve."

"But we also have more community support than we realized," Lauren pointed out. "Tom, Ray, Wade, Matt. Plus, countless others in town. We're not facing this alone."

As they prepared for the confrontation ahead, Jackie reflected on how the investigation had revealed not just criminal conspiracy but also the strength of connections they'd built in Prairie Rose. Wade Brooks' apology represented more than just clearing a suspect. It showed how crisis could lead to understanding and how community bonds could survive even serious misunderstandings.

Now they just had to survive long enough to fully enjoy those connections.

Chapter Twenty

Prairie Rose Cemetery sat on a gentle hill overlooking the town, its weathered headstones and ancient oak trees creating the kind of peaceful setting that made death seem like a natural transition rather than an ending. Under different circumstances, Jackie might have found comfort in the quiet dignity of the place where Uncle Charlie Joe rested beside his mentor Ezra Hutchins.

But at 11:00 PM, with federal agents positioning themselves throughout the cemetery and a desperate criminal planning ambush, the peaceful setting felt more like a battlefield waiting for war to begin.

"Radio check," Agent Reeves's voice crackled through Jackie's earpiece. "All units report status."

Jackie listened as tactical teams, snipers, and surveillance units confirmed their positions around the cemetery perimeter. The level of coordination was impressive, but she couldn't shake the feeling that Zoe Vonn had anticipated this kind of response.

"Remember," Agent Reeves continued, "our primary objective is capturing Zoe Vonn alive so we can identify and arrest the remaining network members. Secondary objective is protecting civilian lives. Do not engage unless she presents an immediate threat."

Jackie adjusted the Kevlar vest under her jacket and checked her watch. One hour until the meeting time, and her nerves were stretched tight with anticipation and fear.

Sheriff Martinez approached their position behind the cemetery's maintenance shed, his expression mixing professional focus with personal concern that was clearly centered on Lauren.

"Agent Reeves wants to review the final approach protocol," he said to Jackie and Melody. "Can you give us a few minutes?"

Jackie caught the meaningful look he directed toward Lauren and realized he wanted privacy for a personal conversation before the operation began.

"Come on, Melody," she said diplomatically. "Let's go check the communication equipment one more time."

After Jackie and Melody moved toward the command post, Ray turned to Lauren, his hand finding hers.

"Lauren," he said quietly, "I need you to promise me you'll be careful in there. Stay close to your sisters, follow every protocol Agent Reeves outlined, and don't take any unnecessary risks."

"I will," Lauren said, squeezing his hand. "We have good backup, and we'll be careful."

Ray stepped closer, his other hand gently touching her face. "I love you," he said simply. "I needed to say that again before you go in there. I love you, and I need you to come back to me safe."

"I love you too," Lauren replied, her voice steady despite the fear in her eyes. "And I promise I'll be careful. We all will."

Ray pulled her close for a brief, gentle kiss. "When this is over, we're going to have that quiet dinner and talk about normal things, okay?"

"I'd like that very much," Lauren said softly.

A discreet cough from behind them indicated that their privacy was ending. Agent Reeves approached with Jackie and Melody, all of them tactfully avoiding direct eye contact to give Ray and Lauren a moment to compose themselves.

"Sorry to interrupt," Agent Reeves said diplomatically, "but we need to move into final positions. Zoe's deadline is in thirty minutes."

Ray straightened, his professional demeanor returning, but his hand found Lauren's and squeezed it gently. "You don't have to do this," he said quietly. "We can still send in a decoy; someone trained for this kind of situation."

"Yes, I do," Lauren replied, surprising everyone by her firm tone. "Zoe specifically asked for us, but she's threatening innocent children if we don't comply. I won't let kids get hurt because we were afraid to face her."

"Plus, she'll know," Jackie said, joining the conversation. "Zoe Vonn has been watching us for weeks so she knows what we look like, how I move, probably even what I sound like. A decoy would be spotted immediately."

Ray looked between the sisters, clearly wanting to argue but recognizing the logic of their position. "Then we make sure you have every possible protection. Full tactical support, constant communication, extraction plan ready if anything goes wrong."

"Ray," Lauren said gently, understanding that his protectiveness was intensified by their feelings for each other. "We'll be careful. We have the best backup possible. And we'll all come home safe."

Ray nodded reluctantly. "Be safe," he said quietly. "Come back to me."

"I will," Lauren promised. "I have too much to live for now to take any unnecessary risks."

He squeezed her hand before moving away to take his position in the shadows.

"Okay. Final positions in fifteen minutes," Agent Reeves announced. "All units ready?"

"We're ready," Jackie said, looking at Lauren and Melody. "We do this together. Jackie's negotiation skills, Melody's analysis, Lauren's calm presence. We use our strengths as a team."

"Agreed," Lauren said firmly, her newfound certainty about Ray giving her additional strength for what lay ahead.

"Statistical probability of success increases significantly with coordinated approach," Melody confirmed.

Ray straightened, his professional demeanor returning. "You have full tactical support, constant communication, and extraction ready if anything goes wrong. Be safe, all of you."

They were then left alone. Jackie looked at her sister and niece as half-part fear and adrenaline rushed through her.

"She might already be here," Jackie said, scanning the cemetery for any signs of movement among the headstones. "Zoe's had all day to get into position."

"Or she's planning to approach from an angle we haven't anticipated," Lauren added.

"Five minutes to midnight," Agent Reeves's voice came through the earpiece. "All units maintain cover and await my signal."

The three women walked toward Uncle Charlie Joe's grave, their footsteps measured and purposeful in the cemetery quiet. The headstone was simple granite with his name, dates, and the inscription "He Fed His Community." Even facing potential death, Jackie felt a moment of pride in the legacy he'd left behind.

They positioned themselves beside the grave, Jackie in the center with Lauren and Melody flanking her. Somewhere in the darkness, Zoe Vonn was watching, planning her move. Somewhere else, federal agents were ready to respond. But for this moment, they stood together with their uncle's memory and their own courage.

"Very touching," a voice said from behind a large memorial stone about twenty feet away. "The devoted family paying respect to the uncle they barely knew."

Zoe Vonn stepped into view, and Jackie was struck by how ordinary she looked, just a middle-aged woman in dark clothes, someone you might pass on the street without a second glance. Only her eyes revealed the calculated intelligence that had helped build a multi-million-dollar criminal empire.

"Zoe Vonn," Jackie said, immediately shifting into her attorney mode. Her voice was steady, posture confident, mind focused on controlling the conversation. "I assume you want to discuss terms for ending this conflict."

"Terms?" Zoe laughed, a sound that carried no humor. "There are no terms. There's only consequences for people who destroy other people's life's work."

"Your life's work was built on corruption and murder," Jackie replied, using the direct confrontational technique that had served her well in depositions. "Tex Morrison. James Morrison. How many others?"

"People who couldn't mind their own business," Zoe moved closer, and Jackie could see she was holding something in her right hand. "People like you and your meddling family."

Melody stepped forward slightly, her analytical mind immediately assessing the situation. "Your organizational structure has completely collapsed," she said with clinical precision. "Lou Paxton's deceased, financial networks compromised, operational assets frozen or confiscated. Continuation of hostile activities serves no strategic purpose."

Zoe's eyes narrowed at Melody's systematic assessment. "Smart girl. Too smart for her own good."

"The FBI has dismantled your organization," Jackie continued, maintaining her negotiation stance. "Your options are limited to surrender and cooperation, or escalation that can only result in your capture or death."

"It's over when I say it's over," Zoe replied. "And I say it ends with the people who started it."

Lauren stepped forward, her voice carrying the patient, calming tone she used with difficult customers. It was a kind of steady presence that could de-escalate tense situations. "We didn't start anything, Zoe. We just wanted justice for a friend. But this doesn't have to end with more violence. You still have choices."

"Justice," Zoe spat the word like a curse. "You wanted to play detective, to feel important, to stick your noses into business that had nothing to do with you."

"Actually," Melody interjected, her systematic mind working through the conversation, "our investigation was methodical and evidence-based. We followed logical patterns of criminal behavior to their inevitable conclusion. Your operation was always going to be discovered eventually."

Jackie recognized Melody's strategy, using analytical reasoning to undermine Zoe's sense of control. "She's right," Jackie added, pressing the negotiation advantage. "Your network was unsustainable. Too many participants, too many moving parts, too many opportunities for exposure. We just happened to be the catalyst."

"You think you understand what we built?" Zoe's voice carried mounting frustration.

"I understand criminal enterprises," Jackie said with professional confidence. "I've prosecuted enough of them. Profit margins, risk assessment, organizational vulnerabilities. It's all predictable once you understand the patterns."

Lauren maintained her calm presence, watching Zoe's body language for signs of escalation while keeping her voice steady. "Zoe, you're angry, and you have a right to be. Your life's work is gone. But taking that anger out on us won't restore what you've lost."

"It'll make me feel better," Zoe said, and Jackie saw her hand move to reveal a gun.

"No," Melody said matter-of-factly, "it won't. Revenge killings provide temporary emotional satisfaction but no lasting resolution of underlying issues. Plus, you're surrounded by federal agents. Statistical probability of successful escape after committing murder is essentially zero."

Jackie saw an opening and pressed it. "Zoe, as an attorney, I can tell you that your situation, while serious, isn't hopeless. Cooperation with federal authorities, testimony against remaining network members, acceptance of responsibility, these actions could significantly impact your sentencing."

"You're negotiating with me?" Zoe seemed genuinely surprised.

"I'm offering you professional legal perspective on your options," Jackie replied smoothly. "Right now, you're facing charges related to the existing conspiracy. Murder charges would change your situation dramatically."

Lauren nodded supportively. "You still have time to make a different choice. No one else has to die tonight."

Before Zoe could respond, multiple spotlights blazed to life around the cemetery.

"Federal agents! Drop your weapon and put your hands in the air!"

Instead of complying, Zoe raised her gun toward the three women. In that instant, all their individual strengths came together; Jackie's quick legal mind assessing options, Melody's analytical brain calculating trajectories and timing, Lauren's calm presence keeping them coordinated.

"Down!" Jackie shouted, her negotiation training having taught her to recognize when talk had failed.

All three women dropped behind Uncle Charlie Joe's granite marker as gunfire erupted around them. The federal response was immediate and overwhelming with tactical teams converging from multiple directions while snipers engaged Zoe's position.

"Stay together!" Lauren called out, her natural calm helping coordinate their movements as they took cover.

"She's moving northeast," Melody observed, tracking Zoe's position with systematic precision. "Using headstones for cover, approximately forty meters from our position."

Jackie's legal mind was already processing what had just occurred. "Everything she said was recorded. Federal agents witnessed her threatening us with a deadly weapon. Whatever happens now, we have a solid case."

The gunfire stopped abruptly, followed by shouted commands from tactical teams.

"Target down," a voice reported through Jackie's earpiece. "Scene secure."

The three women remained pressed against Uncle Charlie Joe's headstone until Agent Reeves appeared and helped them to their feet. Across the cemetery, paramedics were working on Zoe Vonn while other agents secured the area.

"Is she alive?" Jackie asked.

"Wounded but stable. She'll survive to stand trial, which is more than can be said for some of her victims."

As the immediate crisis passed, Jackie realized how effectively they'd worked together during the confrontation. Each had contributed their unique strengths with Jackie's negotiation keeping Zoe talking and revealing information, Melody's analysis undermining Zoe's confidence and tactical position, Lauren's calm presence maintaining their coordination under pressure.

Ray appeared at Lauren's side as soon as the scene was declared safe, his relief evident as he briefly squeezed her hand.

"You kept your promise," he said quietly.

"We all did," Lauren replied, looking at Jackie and Melody with pride.

"We used our individual strengths as a coordinated team," Melody observed with satisfaction. "Optimal approach for managing hostile negotiations."

"It's really over now, isn't it?" Lauren asked.

"This part is over," Agent Reeves confirmed. "We'll need weeks to completely dismantle the network and prosecute all the participants, but the immediate threat to your family and community has been eliminated."

As they prepared to leave the cemetery, Jackie paused at Uncle Charlie Joe's headstone. The granite was chipped from gunfire, but the inscription was still clearly visible: "He Fed His Community."

"Thank you," she said quietly, not caring who heard her speaking to a grave. "For bringing us together, for teaching us what matters, and for helping us be brave enough to protect what you built."

The drive back to the restaurant was subdued, weighted with exhaustion and the aftermath of violence. But as they approached their home, Jackie felt a deep sense of completion. They'd honored Tex Morrison's memory, protected their community from corruption, and proved that Uncle Charlie Joe's faith in their family had been justified.

"What happens now?" Lauren asked as they settled into their apartment above the restaurant.

"Now we go back to serving barbecue and taking care of our community," Jackie said. "That's what Uncle Charlie Joe would want."

"And we remember that sometimes justice requires ordinary people to do extraordinary things," Melody added.

"And we remember that family is worth fighting for," Lauren concluded.

As they prepared for what they hoped would be their first peaceful night's sleep in weeks, Jackie reflected on how much their lives had changed.

Uncle Charlie Joe's legacy lived on, not just in the restaurant he'd built, but in the family he'd brought together and the courage he'd inspired them to find within themselves.

Tomorrow they would return to their normal routine of smoking brisket, serving customers, and being part of Prairie Rose's daily life. But they would do it with the knowledge that they'd proven themselves worthy of the trust their community had placed in them.

The investigation was over, the criminals were defeated, and the Rodriguez women were home where they belonged.

Chapter Twenty-One

Three weeks after the final arrest, life at Charlie Joe's BBQ Shack had settled into a peaceful rhythm that felt both familiar and wonderfully normal. The media attention had faded, the FBI had finished their paperwork, and the restaurant was once again focused on what it did best: serving excellent barbecue to a community that had become family.

Melody sat at her favorite corner table, laptop open, working on her application essays for forensic science programs. Aiden was beside her with his own laptop, helping her research graduate school options while simultaneously analyzing data patterns for a consulting project he'd taken on with the local sheriff's department.

Aiden's weekend visit had started to become a regular occurrence. When he was home in San Antonio the pair spoke daily via FaceTime.

Blue lay contentedly between their chairs, his head resting on Melody's feet in the position that had become his standard afternoon routine. The dog's presence had become such a natural part of Melody's daily life that she unconsciously planned her workspace around accommodating him.

"The University of North Texas has an excellent forensic science program," Aiden said, turning his screen toward her. "And it's close enough that we could both attend. They have research opportunities in digital forensics that would be perfect for my interests."

"The methodology courses look comprehensive," Melody agreed, studying the curriculum. "And they have specialized tracks for crime scene analysis and laboratory techniques."

Lauren approached with coffee refills, pausing to watch how naturally Melody worked with Blue's calming presence. Over the past few weeks, she'd observed her daughter's increased confidence, improved stress management, and growing comfort with social interactions, much of which seemed connected to the therapeutic relationship with Blue.

"You two look settled," Lauren said, settling into a nearby chair. "Like you've found your rhythm."

"We have," Melody said simply. "Aiden understands how I process information, and Blue provides stability during complex analytical work. It's an efficient partnership."

"Speaking of partnerships," Lauren said carefully, "I've been thinking about something. Melody, how would you feel about having your own dog?"

Both Melody and Aiden looked up with immediate interest.

"My own dog?" Melody asked, her analytical mind immediately beginning to process the implications. "For therapeutic support purposes, or as a companion animal?"

"Both," Lauren replied. "Blue has been so helpful for you during the investigation and afterward. But he belongs to Tom, and he has his own work responsibilities. I thought you might benefit from having a dog that's specifically trained to support your needs."

Tom appeared from the kitchen where he'd been helping Jovie with an equipment repair, Blue immediately alerting to his presence but remaining in position beside Melody.

"Did I hear something about dogs?" Tom asked, wiping his hands on a towel.

"Mom's suggesting I should get my own dog," Melody explained. "For therapeutic support and companionship."

Tom's weathered face broke into a genuine smile. "That's an excellent idea. Blue's shown us just how much difference the right dog can make for someone with your particular strengths and needs."

"You think it would be appropriate?" Melody asked, her systematic mind already working through logistics. "I'd need to research training requirements, space considerations, care responsibilities..."

"I know someone who might be perfect for you," Tom said, settling into a chair with them. "My cousin rescues and raises dogs specifically for therapy and assistance work. He's got a young female, about eight months old, who's been through basic training and shows real aptitude for emotional support work."

Aiden leaned forward with interest. "What kind of training does she have?"

"Foundation obedience, stress recognition, calming techniques, and some specialized skills for supporting people with sensory processing differences. The dog's been socialized specifically for working with individuals who need consistent, predictable support patterns."

"That sounds... ideal," Melody said, her voice carrying the careful tone she used when something felt almost too good to believe. "But the financial considerations, the time commitment, the adjustment period..."

"Melody," Lauren said gently, "you've shown incredible growth and confidence over the past six months. You've contributed to solving two murder investigations, you're planning for graduate school, and you're building a relationship with Aiden. You've proven you can handle major life changes and responsibilities."

"Plus," Aiden added, "having your own trained companion would give you independence while providing support. It would be your partnership, developed according to your specific needs and preferences."

Blue's tail thumped against the floor, as if approving of the discussion. The dog had remained calmly positioned throughout the conversation, providing his usual steady presence while the humans planned for Melody's future.

"Tom," Melody said, her decision-making process reaching its systematic conclusion, "could we arrange to meet this dog? I'd like to assess compatibility and training levels before making a commitment."

"Of course," Tom replied. "My cousin's place is about an hour drive from here. We could go next weekend if you'd like."

"I'd like to come too," Aiden said immediately. "If that's appropriate. I want to understand how to support both you and your dog in our future plans."

Melody felt warmth spread through her chest, the same pleasant sensation that had become associated with Aiden's thoughtful consideration of her needs. "I'd like that very much. Having your analytical perspective during the selection process would be valuable."

Lauren watched her daughter with deep satisfaction. Six months ago, Melody had been isolated and uncertain about her future. Now she was making plans for graduate school, building a romantic relationship, and considering taking responsibility for her own therapeutic companion.

Perhaps she would even learn to drive the way Aiden does. The possibility that her daughter had a different future than she originally imagined excited her.

"This is really happening, isn't it?" Lauren said quietly. "You're building an independent life while staying connected to family."

"Statistical analysis suggests that structured support systems combined with appropriate companionship significantly improve long-term outcomes for individuals with my neurological profile," Melody replied matter-of-factly. Then she smiled, an expression that had become more frequent and genuine over recent months. "But in simpler terms, yes. I think I'm ready to build my own life while keeping the family connections that matter."

Blue stretched contentedly, adjusted his position to maintain contact with Melody's feet, and settled back into his afternoon nap. Even he seemed to approve of the plans being made around him.

Lauren returned to the kitchen and Tom went to start his afternoon demonstration. Melody and Aiden moved outside to continue their research from the picnic table with a clear view of Blue working.

Minutes later, the familiar sound of Sheriff Martinez's patrol car pulling into the lot drew Jackie's attention away from Tom's demonstration. Through the kitchen window, she could see Lauren's face light up as she spotted Ray walking toward the restaurant, and Jackie couldn't help but smile at her sister's obvious happiness.

Ray entered through the back door, moving with the easy familiarity of someone who'd become part of the daily routine. He was in uniform but off duty, his relaxed posture and warm smile indicating this was a personal visit.

"Afternoon, Jackie," he said, touching his hat brim in greeting. "Finished my shift early and thought I'd stop by to see if you needed any help with the weekend crowd."

"Ray!" Lauren's smile was brilliant as she emerged from the kitchen, wiping her hands on her apron. "I wasn't expecting you until this evening."

Lauren said, standing on her tiptoes to give him a quick kiss that spoke of comfortable intimacy.

"Put me to work," Ray said immediately, already moving toward the hand-washing station and tying on one of their extra aprons. A sight that should have looked ridiculous on a uniformed sheriff but somehow seemed perfectly natural on him.

"If you really want to help, I could use another pair of hands with the serving line."

"Perfect," he said.

Jackie watched with amusement as Ray seamlessly integrated into their lunch service routine, portioning coleslaw with practiced efficiency and taking orders to tables with the kind of personal attention that showed he'd been learning their customer service approach.

"Ray, can you grab the coleslaw from the walk-in?" Lauren called out as she plated brisket for a waiting customer. "We're running low up front."

"On it," Ray replied, disappearing into the cooler and returning with a large container. But instead of just setting it down, he began portioning the slaw into serving trays with the practiced efficiency of someone who'd been watching Lauren's methods and learning her systems.

The easy banter between them was interrupted by the sound of a car door slamming in the parking lot, followed by the distinctive click of high heels on gravel. Jackie glanced through the kitchen window and felt her stomach drop.

"Oh no," she muttered.

"What?" Lauren asked, following Jackie's gaze to see an impeccably dressed woman in her seventies approaching the front door with the determined stride of someone who owned every room she entered.

"That's Mom," Jackie said grimly.

Dawn Rodriguez swept through the front door of the restaurant like a force of nature, taking in the crowded dining room, Tom's herding demonstration visible through the back windows, and the general controlled chaos of a busy Saturday with sharp, appraising eyes.

"Well," she announced to no one in particular, "this is certainly... rustic."

Ray looked between Lauren and Jackie, immediately sensing the tension that had filled the kitchen. "Should I … um, go?"

"No, stay," Lauren said quickly, her voice tight with sudden anxiety.

Dawn made her way to the kitchen, navigating around busy servers and occupied tables with the practiced ease of someone accustomed to making dramatic entrances. She was dressed as if she were attending a country club luncheon rather than visiting a barbecue restaurant, complete with pearl earrings and a handbag that probably cost more than most people's monthly salary.

"I hope you don't mind the unexpected visit," Dawn said, though her tone suggested she didn't particularly care if they minded or not. "I was driving back from San Antonio and thought I'd finally see this restaurant everyone's been talking about."

"I asked you to call in advance," Jackie said firmly, not pausing in her plating of a brisket sandwich. "We're in the middle of our busiest service of the day."

"Oh, I'm sure you can spare a few minutes for your mother," Dawn replied, then her gaze landed on Ray, who was standing beside Lauren wearing an apron and holding a serving spoon. Her expression shifted from casual superiority to complete bewilderment. "And who might this be?"

Lauren's cheeks flushed pink, her hands trembling slightly as she tried to maintain her composure during the lunch rush. "Mom, this is Sheriff Ray Martinez. Ray, this is my mother, Dawn Rodriguez."

Ray immediately stepped forward, extending his hand despite the awkward circumstances. "Pleasure to meet you, Mrs. Rodriguez."

Dawn's eyebrows rose as she took in Ray's uniform visible beneath the apron, the easy way he stood beside Lauren, and the obvious familiarity with their kitchen operations. "Sheriff Martinez. How... interesting. Are you here in an official capacity?"

"He's here because he's my boyfriend and he's helping with the lunch rush," Lauren said, her voice carrying a note of defiance that reminded Jackie of their teenage years.

"Boyfriend?" Dawn's voice went up an octave, her carefully composed expression cracking with shock. "Lauren, dear, when were you planning to mention this... development?"

The kitchen fell silent except for the sizzling from the grill. Jackie could see other customers glancing toward them with interest, and Jovie had stopped working entirely to watch the family drama unfold.

"Since we don't talk, and haven't in years, I didn't think it was worth mentioning," Lauren said coolly.

"Well, Jackie and I speak so she could have told me." Her words cutting through Jackie like a knife. Jackie was questioning why she'd ever sided with her mother all those years ago. She now saw her through different eyes.

"Mrs. Rodriguez," Ray interjected diplomatically, "perhaps this conversation would be better saved for after the lunch service?"

"Actually, I'd love to stay and observe," Dawn said, settling herself at the counter where she could watch the kitchen operations. "I'm clearly very behind on my daughters' lives. This is... illuminating."

Jackie felt her jaw clench at her mother's tone, but before she could respond, Melody appeared from the dining room carrying a tray of empty plates.

"Grandmother Rodriguez," Melody said with her characteristic directness. "Your arrival timing coincides with our peak service period. Statistical analysis shows that family emotional discussions during high-stress operational periods reduce efficiency by an average of thirty-seven percent."

Dawn stared at her granddaughter, clearly taken aback by both Melody's blunt assessment and how much she'd grown since their last meeting. "Hello, Melody. It's... lovely to see you too."

"Order up!" Jovie called from the smoker station, apparently trying to restore some normalcy to the disrupted kitchen. "Three pulled pork plates!"

Ray immediately moved to collect the plates, but Dawn's presence had clearly disrupted the smooth workflow they'd established. Lauren was struggling to keep up with orders while processing her mother's unexpected appearance and obvious shock about Ray.

"So, this is how you make your living now?" Dawn asked Lauren, watching as she fumbled with a serving spoon. "Serving barbecue in a small town? With a... boyfriend?"

"We're serving excellent food to a community that's become family," Lauren replied, her voice tight with controlled emotion. "And Ray helps because he cares about what matters to me."

"I see. And how long has this... relationship been going on?" Her eyes cutting over to stare at Jackie, even though the question was directed to Lauren.

"Mrs. Rodriguez," Ray said quietly, setting down his dish towel and approaching Dawn with the calm authority he used in difficult law enforcement situations, "I can see you're interested in your daughters' work. Would you like me to give you a tour of the restaurant and explain some of the operations? That way Lauren and Jackie can focus on their customers."

It was a diplomatic solution that removed Dawn from the kitchen workspace while showing respect for her interest. Jackie felt a surge of gratitude for Ray's quick thinking and social skills.

"That would be lovely," Dawn said, clearly pleased by the attention and curious to learn more about this man she'd never heard of. "I'd be very interested in your perspective on their... business practices."

As Ray guided Dawn toward the dining room, Lauren caught his eye and mouthed "thank you." He winked in return, then began explaining their customer service philosophy to Dawn in terms that emphasized the sisters' expertise and success.

"Is she always like that?" Melody asked after they'd left.

"Unfortunately, yes," Lauren replied, her shoulders sagging with relief now that the immediate pressure was gone. "Mom has never learned the difference between helpful suggestions and criticism disguised as concern."

"Her timing is statistically improbable," Melody observed. "The likelihood of a random visit occurring during our busiest service period suggests either poor planning or deliberate choice."

"Deliberate choice," Jackie said grimly as they rushed to catch up on orders. "Mom likes to create dramatic moments. It gives her more control over the situation and more material to critique later."

They managed to finish the lunch service without further disruption, though Jackie could hear Dawn's voice from the dining room as Ray patiently answered her questions about restaurant operations, local law enforcement, and his relationship with Lauren.

"Mrs. Rodriguez says to tell you the brisket is perfect," Ray reported when he returned to the kitchen an hour later, looking slightly drained but professionally composed. "And she's very interested in meeting with both of you after the afternoon crowd dies down."

"I bet she is," Jackie muttered, then looked at Ray with genuine appreciation. "Thank you for handling that. You didn't have to field an interrogation from my mother about your relationship with Lauren."

"Actually, it was kind of nice," Ray said with a slight smile. "She clearly loves you both, even if her way of showing it is... complicated. And she's very proud of what you've built here, though she'd probably never say it directly."

Lauren looked skeptical. "Did she say that?"

"Not in so many words. But she spent twenty minutes asking detailed questions about your customer base, your operational efficiency, and your role in the community. That's not the behavior of someone who disapproves. That's someone trying to understand something important to her daughters."

After Dawn finally left two hours later with promises to "call ahead next time" and an invitation for Ray to visit her in Austin, the restaurant felt noticeably more peaceful. Jackie, Lauren, and Melody settled on the front porch with Melody and Aiden, who had arrived during the family drama and wisely stayed in the background.

"Well," Lauren said finally, "that was unexpected."

"Your mother is formidable," Aiden observed diplomatically. "Melody's statistical analysis of family disruption patterns was very accurate."

"Thank you," Melody said. "Though I should note that Grandmother Rodriguez's surprise about Ray suggests significant communication gaps in our family structure."

"We're working on that," Jackie said. "Some family relationships take time to rebuild."

"Yes and based on today, I'm not in a hurry to rebuild with her just yet," Lauren said flatly.

They were joined by Matt Klein, who approached with a plate of brisket and a satisfied expression. "Heard you had some family excitement today. Hope everything's okay."

"Just our mother making one of her dramatic appearances," Jackie replied. "Nothing we couldn't handle."

"Good to hear. Charles would be proud of how you handled family pressure while maintaining restaurant operations," Matt said. "That's not easy to do."

"The systematic management was impressive," Emma Barber said, joining them on the porch with a tray of what appeared to be individual dessert portions. "I watched from the kitchen during the family drama, and nobody missed a beat with customer service despite the disruption."

"Emma," Lauren said warmly, "I didn't realize you were here during Mom's visit."

"I arrived right when she did, actually. Figured it was better to stay in the background until things calmed down." Emma set her tray on the porch table, revealing what looked like small ramekins of panna cotta garnished with fresh herbs. "I was testing this new lemon-thyme dessert recipe while you dealt with the family situation."

Jackie tasted the dessert and found it perfectly balanced, light and refreshing after a heavy barbecue meal, with subtle flavors that complemented rather than competed with their food. "This is excellent. How did you develop the recipe?"

"Recovery taught me to pay attention to how different foods affect energy levels and digestion," Emma said matter-of-factly. "Turns out that kind of analysis translates well to menu development. Plus, watching Mom work taught me that the best restaurant desserts enhance the entire meal experience rather than overwhelming it."

Jovie appeared from the kitchen, automatically checking on her daughter's well-being while trying not to be obvious about it. "Emma, you've been on your feet for over four hours today. How are you feeling?"

"Actually, feeling really good, Mom. Strong enough to work through family drama, strong enough to perfect a new recipe, strong enough to be part of the daily operations instead of just visiting occasionally." Emma's smile was radiant. "Good enough to contribute to our family business."

Jackie felt moved by the simple pride in Emma's voice. The young woman had fought her way back from life-threatening illness to become an integral part of their restaurant family, bringing her own skills and perspective to their collaborative efforts.

"Our family business," Jovie repeated softly, and Jackie could see the profound gratitude in her eyes, not just for Emma's recovery, but for the community that had welcomed them both completely.

"So, I'm officially part of the team now?" Emma asked the group.

"Anyone who can develop recipes this good while helping maintain kitchen operations during family crises is definitely team material," Jackie replied.

As the evening settled over Prairie Rose and their extended family began to disperse, Jackie found herself on the porch with just Lauren and Melody, finally able to process the day's events without Dawn's watchful presence.

"So," Lauren said, settling into her chair with a tired sigh, "I guess Ray passed the family introduction test."

"He handled Mom beautifully," Jackie agreed. "Professional, respectful, but he didn't let her intimidate him or make him defensive about your relationship."

"I was so embarrassed," Lauren admitted. "Having her show up like that, finding out about Ray in front of everyone, making that scene during lunch service."

"Ray didn't seem embarrassed," Melody observed. "His response patterns suggested he was focused on conflict resolution rather than personal discomfort. That's a positive indicator for relationship stability."

Lauren smiled at her daughter's clinical assessment. "Are you saying you approve of him?"

"I'm saying his behavioral responses under stress suggest he's committed to family harmony rather than personal ego protection. That's statistically correlated with successful long-term partnerships."

"I'll take that as approval," Lauren laughed.

As they prepared to head upstairs to their apartment, Jackie looked around at the life they'd built, at their thriving restaurant, the strong community connections, the family relationships that had weathered even Dawn's unexpected visit.

"You know," she said, "today actually went pretty well. We handled the lunch rush, dealt with family drama, and nobody killed anybody."

"Ray really did fit right in," Lauren agreed. "Even with Mom's surprise interrogation."

"Speaking of fitting in," Melody said, "Aiden's integration into our community activities has been very successful. His forensic science insights add value to our educational programming."

"And speaking of relationships," Lauren said with a knowing look at Jackie. "Looks like everyone's finding their path forward."

"Everyone except Jackie," Melody observed with her characteristic directness.

"I guess we'll just need to find someone for her now," Lauren said with a laugh.

THE END

Before you go: If you loved Grilled Corruption, be sure to visit my website to sign up for my newsletter and to stay up to date on new releases and other bookish things. When signing up, you can pick either Unsolved Murder prequel to my Medium with a Heart series or the Alphabet Soup Recipe from my Alphabet Soup Mysteries series. Either are a win.

Continue to the next section for this book's recipe!

www.ejwheltonwrites.com

Recipe:

While I didn't mention ambrosia in this book, it is still something I always think of when it comes to barbecue. There is a local restaurant where we would get catering and one of the sides was always ambrosia. Or when we would grill burgers and hot dogs for things like the Fourth of July or Memorial Day, this was a dish somebody would bring.

I also had wanted to tweak the recipe to be something different, not the standard, but you know what, the plain standard recipe is the absolute best! So, this is just that.

Ambrosia:

3 cans (15 oz) Fruit Cocktail in light syrup (I get the extra cherries one)
1 can (15 oz) Mandarian oranges
1 can (8 oz) Pineapple tidbits (or really any, but you want bits)
1 cup shredded coconut (sweetened)
½ bag mini marshmallows (more if you like more)
½ cup sour cream
1 tub (15 oz) whipped topping

Drain all the fruit to get all the juice/liquid out.
Add to a bowl with the remaining ingredients. Mix well.
Chill in refrigerator for at least 4 hours (or longer), stirring occasionally. Enjoy as a side dish or dessert!!

Author note:

I love this series! I don't know what else to say about it. This one was fun to write for a lot of reasons. We continue to follow along with the family's progress as they learn about barbecue and cooking as well as working together.

Melody continues to be inspired by my grandsons. When they lived with me, I know my dogs were a comfort to them at times. They have three cats now and they provide a level of comfort to them as well.

As for the cooking competition in this story, it was inspired by stories my husband has shared with me about his time (before we had met) when he competed in cook-offs. He has been a rock for questions about temps and smells and how competitions work.

And finally, I want to thank you the readers for following me on this journey. I hope you will stick around for the next in this series which is Marinated Lies. This one's theme is also inspired by my husband and his (former) motorcycle riding club.

www.ejwheltonwrites.com